WE
CAN
BE
HEROES

Also by Kyrie McCauley
If These Wings Can Fly

WE
CAN
BE
HEROES

KYRIE McCAULEY

KATHERINE TEGEN BOOKS
An Imprint of HarperCollins Publishers

Katherine Tegen Books is an imprint of HarperCollins Publishers.

We Can Be Heroes
Copyright © 2021 by Kyrie McCauley
All rights reserved. Printed in the United States of America.
No part of this book may be used or reproduced in any manner whatsoever
without written permission except in the case of brief quotations embodied in
critical articles and reviews. For information address HarperCollins
Children's Books, a division of HarperCollins Publishers,
195 Broadway, New York, NY 10007.
www.epicreads.com

Library of Congress Cataloging-in-Publication Data

Names: McCauley, Kyrie, author.
Title: We can be heroes / Kyrie McCauley.
Description: First edition. | New York, NY : Katherine Tegen Books, [2021]
| Audience: Ages 13 & up. | Audience: Grades 10–12. | Summary: "After a
girl is killed by her ex-boyfriend in a school shooting, her two best
friends attempt to memorialize her in a town economically dependent on
the shooter's family"— Provided by publisher.
Identifiers: LCCN 2021016819 | ISBN 978-0-06-288505-0 (hardcover)
Subjects: CYAC: School shootings—Fiction. | Gun control—Fiction. | Dating
violence—Fiction. | Social media—Fiction. | Mural painting and
decoration—Fiction. | Ghosts—Fiction.
Classification: LCC PZ7.1.M42213 We 2021 | DDC [Fic]—dc23
LC record available at https://lccn.loc.gov/2021016819

Typography by Joel Tippie
21 22 23 24 25   PC/LSCH   10 9 8 7 6 5 4 3 2 1
❖
First Edition

For girls who are told that they're too much for this world.
Too loud, too opinionated, too sensitive, too angry.
You are exactly the right amount for the right people.
Find them and let them love all too much of you.

And for Andrew, Rowan & Theo.
Thank you for loving all too much of me.

WE CAN BE HEROES
SEASON 2: EPISODE 13
"THE SHERIFF"

MERIT LOGAN: Welcome, listeners, to We Can Be Heroes, *a podcast made for survivors of violence in the tradition of the "Take Back the Night" rallies that began in the 1970s and continue to this day. I'm your host, Merit Logan. This season, we will be aiming our lens at gun violence as it relates to gender-based violence. Really, though, our series begins with the story of one young woman, Cassandra Queen.*

[Audio clip]
911 Dispatcher: 911. What's your emergency?
Caller: Someone has a gun. We heard shots.
911 Dispatcher: Can you tell me where you are calling from?
Caller: The high school. We're at school. There's someone shooting.
SHERIFF THOMAS: It was the worst day of my career, bar none. It's the kind of call we're all dreading these days. Active shooter. Calls coming from Bell High School. Our operators got overwhelmed in seconds, with all those kids and their cells. Then the panicked parent calls started coming in, too.

MERIT LOGAN: You just heard from the sheriff of Bell, a town that has been called "the heart of American gun culture"—it happens to be my hometown, and it's going to serve as a case study for us to look at gun violence these next few weeks. This is the town where Bell Firearms has been owned and operated from for nearly two hundred years. Bell is also the place where just five months ago, Nicolas Bell, heir to Bell Firearms and fortune, took his father's guns to school and murdered his ex-girlfriend, seventeen-year-old Cassandra Queen.

MERIT: Sheriff Thomas, do you know how many women are shot to death by current or former intimate partners each month in this country?

SHERIFF THOMAS: I don't have those statistics in front of—

MERIT: Okay, fair enough. In your *personal* knowledge, then, when you train your officers on responding to domestic disputes—mainly incidents of domestic violence—what do you tell them?

SHERIFF THOMAS: To never go alone. Be prepared for that violence to turn on them. Domestics are some of the deadliest calls officers can respond to.

MERIT: Yes, they are. That lines up with national data . . . but you didn't think Cassie was in imminent danger?

SHERIFF THOMAS: I had no reason to believe she was in danger.

MERIT: Did Cassie think she was in danger?

SHERIFF THOMAS: I can't speak to that, Ms. Logan. I didn't know Cassandra Queen. Or Nicolas Bell, for that matter.

MERIT: But you know his father, Steven Bell.

SHERIFF THOMAS: No comment, Ms. Logan.

MERIT: It wasn't a question, Sheriff Thomas.

[Long pause]

MERIT: Okay, then, can you speak to his access to weapons?

SHERIFF THOMAS: Nico? Everyone has access to guns in this town. It's not a problem.

MERIT: Not a problem? When a girl is dead?

SHERIFF THOMAS: Girls are killed every day, Ms. Logan.

MERIT: But, Sheriff—

SHERIFF THOMAS: It's a *terrible* tragedy, what happened to Cassie Queen—

MERIT: What *did* happen to Cassie? Did she come to you for help—

SHERIFF THOMAS: But it's hardly the gun's fault.

MERIT: Whose fault is it, sir?

MURAL 1

TITLE: CASSANDRA

LOCATION: THE BILLBOARD ON ROUTE 90

BECK

BECK USED TO LIE AWAKE AT night and wish aliens would
abduct her.

She would fall asleep on the fire escape, watching the
night sky. She was desperate for a break in the smoggy
clouds over the city. Eager for a glimpse of the stars. Beck
thought that maybe, if she could see the stars, they could
see her, too.

She used to imagine them beaming her up to their ship.
Their lights too bright. Their huge glossy eyes staring at
her. And she would be the one human. The only one in the
entire world they were looking for. They'd comb long fingers
through her hair and ask to examine her crooked teeth.
They would look past all of the broken parts of her and see
one whole and spectacular creature. And in that moment,
as she imagined it when she was six, she'd be special. Not
just here on Earth, but in a cosmic way. They'd pick *her*,
not despite being forgotten, but because of it.

Who better to explain an entire species than the young it has abandoned?

Who better to seek a new home among the stars?

A drop of sweat reached her eye and Beck blinked at the sting. When that didn't help, she released one hand from the rusted rung of the ladder she was climbing and wiped her forehead, letting her curling hair catch at the wetness and soak it up.

Her other hand slipped on the rung, and she reached back again quickly, steadying her grip on the ladder. Halfway there.

Stop daydreaming, Beck told herself. *And don't look down.*

Beck looked down.

If there had been another surface to work on, one closer to the ground, Beck would have picked that instead. But Bell only has one billboard on Route 90. And twenty-four hours a day, seven days a week, 365 days a year, plus one in a leap year, that sign advertises the only thing this town is known for: Bell Firearms.

Unless you count Cassie.

But no one wants to talk about that.

Beck shifted her backpack, heard the clink of metal on metal as the paint canisters inside fell against each other. When she got to the top she paused, dropping the bag and sitting with her back against the image of the billboard, facing the highway. It was empty. Silent this early in the morning. Beck looked up at the night sky. New moon. No clouds. There were a trillion stars above her, and all of a sudden Beck felt six years old again, small and insignificant. Back before Grandpa pulled her into his universe and gave her a soft place to land. Before Cassie lent her a pencil, and a soft smile, on her first day in a new school.

Beck felt she was back where she had begun. Sitting on a rusty metal grate, staring at the night sky, wondering if there was something—or someone—out there waiting for her. Beck couldn't help the echo of the words she'd thought as a child, when she longed for some sign that she wasn't alone in the universe. *Maybe someday they'll come for me.*

And she couldn't help but wonder if Cassie was out there somewhere now, too.

Tonight's plan was a stupid one, even for Beck. She knew that. She would probably end up arrested, to the surprise of absolutely no one. But the billboard was the last thing you saw leaving Bell, and what was covering it now was a travesty.

Beck craned her neck, taking in the familiar sign with its old typeset font.

Bell Firearms, Established 1824.

Her mask fit snugly against her face, and she pinched the nose to secure it. That was Grandpa's only rule about painting: Be safe. Protect your lungs. Advice that felt like a dagger after his diagnosis.

Beck could feel the expanse of darkness at her back. Her fear of heights was like a hollowness in the balls of her feet.

It was the sensation of falling even though she *knew* she was still standing there, safe, eighteen inches from the edge.

That's the thing about fear, though. You can't convince yourself it doesn't make sense. It's instinct. It's survival.

Cassie should have been more afraid.

The thought tugged Beck's finger on the paint can's trigger, and she started to cover the Bell advertisement with white paint, until it was just a blank canvas. Then she exchanged one can of paint for another, and in bold black lines she outlined the shape of a jaw, a nose, tracing the darkness of her curling hair. She added a bit of blue for her eyes. A pink smudge of her cheeks. Beck painted her as the Greek prophetess, Cassandra—Cassie's namesake—with gold foil leaves feathered in her hair. In the mythology, Cassandra saw what wreckage was coming, but no one listened to her.

Without meaning to, Beck had painted her with a hint of a smile. Cassie, who loved to laugh.

Something twisted inside of her at the memory, quick and wrenching, like a rotary ratchet tightening a bolt.

They said she was smiling when she died.

CASSIE

You don't haunt
the place where you died.
That's only in horror movies,
and Gothic novels.

Ghosts lingering
where they were killed—
where their lives were stolen.
I hate that.
Why would I
ever go back to
that time,
that place?
The one that took
everything from me.

Instead I haunt the place
where I lived,

where I laughed,
the place where some part of me—
a soul? I don't know.
I don't really know
what I believe anymore,
but some piece of me
came back here,
and for months I've been
trying to speak,
to be seen or heard.

But I'm just here, invisible,
in a strange and soft in-between,
neither living nor dead
bored, mostly.

Welcome to the afterlife
of Cassandra Queen.

VIVIAN

THERE WAS BLOOD EVERYWHERE.

Vivian reached for a fresh set of gloves and pulled them so they snapped against her wrists.

"What a mess," Matteo said, filling the bucket.

"It's late, and you have another shift tomorrow. I can clean up," Vivian said, reaching for it, but he held it out of reach.

"Nah, I'll help. It'll go faster," he insisted. He was already rolling the neon-yellow bucket, the one used for hazardous materials. In their line of work, that always meant bodily fluids. Blood.

The call came in ten minutes before the end of their shift. A car wreck. Not the worst crash either of them had ever responded to, but critical when they'd arrived on the scene.

Matteo stopped the bleeding. Vivian started the heart.

Now the back of the ambulance looked like a crime scene instead of the place where someone's life was just saved.

Vivian worked quietly, ringing out the mop again and

again. The blood didn't bother her anymore. Not the scent of it, or the slippery feel of it on her gloves. She pretended it was melted metal. Or spilled oil. Some other slick, precious liquid.

She watched the water as she worked. The way it got less murky brown each time they dumped it, until finally, it ran clean. Washed away as if the night never happened.

If only.

Vivian waved goodbye to Matteo in the parking lot, climbing into her mom's old Civic. She had meant to take the car to college in August. Now she used it to drive to the fire station and back for her shifts.

Vivian's whole head ached from the pull of the too-tight French braids she wore the entire shift, and she wanted nothing more than to tug them loose. But she knew as soon as she let her hair down it would stick to her neck and back, clinging with the July heat.

She ought to cut it off. The same way she'd cut off all the other old parts of her life. Like college. Like her dreams of med school.

Like Beck.

The yellow gas light flashed on when she turned the ignition.

"Dammit," she said, leaning her head against the steering wheel. She glanced at the clock on the dashboard. All the gas stations in town were closed. The only twenty-four-hour station was down the highway, halfway to Tannersville.

But she could make it there on one bar. She'd done it before.

Vivian reached for her phone as she pulled out of the parking lot of the station. She didn't need her mother's voice in her head telling her not to play with her phone and drive—she'd seen enough casualties herself as an EMT. But without music there was a good chance she would doze off at the steering wheel on Route 90. And Vivian had seen those casualties, too.

Vivian used to listen to true-crime podcasts when she drove, but she couldn't anymore. Instead she scrolled to her loudest playlist, some kind of alt-rock screaming monstrosity. It wasn't even hers. It was one of Beck's. Their shared music was usually categorized in her mind as *Never play these or you have to feel things*, but tonight Vivian was grateful for the option. For the loudness of it. The way it drowned out the other things. It dawned on her that this was probably why Beck loved this music. She'd always had memories she'd rather block out.

Vivian had only had them since March.

Either side of the highway was flanked by sunflowers, tall in late summer, with the festival just a few weeks out. Vivian rolled down the windows. The summer heat made the air stagnant and heavy, but she drove fast enough that a slight breeze blew into her car. Even if it wasn't cool, it was something, and it let her smell the sunflowers. They didn't smell sweet like other flowers. They just smelled like the earth. They reminded her of Cassie. When they were little, they'd run through those sunflowers as fast as they could, not caring when the paper-thin leaves cut their arms and faces. They ran like that in recent years, too, but usually only after a few drinks stolen from their parents' liquor cabinets.

Suddenly Vivian spotted a figure on the billboard platform up ahead, and nearly swerved off the road.

Were they going to *jump*? Even if they weren't, they could fall, and that height would hurt them badly.

Vivian pulled off the road. She was out of the car the moment it stopped moving, EMT training kicking in. Training that taught her to use that adrenaline to her advantage. To think and respond faster. Fast enough to save a life.

Training that was more useful than it should have been at the age of eighteen, when five months ago she talked a classmate through tying a tourniquet on her own leg before she lost consciousness.

That was the day Vivian learned that you could have all the training in the world. You still can't save everyone.

But tonight, when she reached the ground below that billboard, Vivian froze, the adrenaline halted at once by shock. It was like she had summoned her with the memory. Not the jumper, who she realized vaguely wasn't a jumper at all, but a *criminal* painting over the billboard.

16

It was the mural that stopped her short.

Vivian recognized the face painted above her immediately. Bold, dark lines of paint shaping her jawline, her ears, her dark hair falling in waves and framed by a gold headband.

And the eyes were just right—a light, icy blue. That curve of a smile that almost never left her face. And one unshed tear, right in the corner of her eye.

The other side of the mural was the thing that killed her: thick lines forming the stark outline of a bullet. On the side of the bullet were four letters: *B-E-L-L.*

Bell Firearms was gone.

Covered up by a portrait of Cassie, and the words in script beneath her: *Collige Virgo Rosas.*

Vivian knew the phrase, but only because Cassie told them once. *It means "Gather, girl, the roses." Pick your flowers, while you still can.*

Cassie had told *them.* When they were all together.

Vivian realized there was only one person who could have done this. Someone she had been avoiding for months.

What was she *thinking?* Vandalism? And she knew how much Beck hated heights.

Only one way to find out.

"Beck!" Vivian shouted. "What are you doing?"

The figure above whirled and dropped a paint canister, which rolled off the edge. Vivian stepped aside as it fell, letting it land harmlessly where she'd been standing.

Beck pulled off her mask and crouched on the platform. "Vivian. You scared the *hell* out of me. Where did you even come from?"

"Work. Get down *now* or I'm calling the cops."

"That's bullshit, even for you. And you know it."

Vivian unlocked her phone, waving the bright screen in the air. "Five! Four!"

"Jesus! Fine! I'm coming."

Beck muttered something under her breath, but Vivian didn't catch it. Probably some foul name. Beck always loved calling her names.

It took several minutes for her to climb down, but then there Beck was, right in front of her. It was the first time they'd been face-to-face since the funeral.

It felt like yesterday.

It felt like a thousand years ago.

"Hey, Vivian," Beck said, her wild red curls breaking out of a messy bun to frame her face. She was covered in sweat and paint, her mask still hanging loose around her neck. Her clothes were stained, but not just from tonight. There was more paint than denim on her overalls.

"Beck," Vivian said. *Typical Beck*, she thought. Doing some stupid, dangerous, unnecessary thing.

But then Vivian looked back at the mural. At Cassie. Vivian knew what it took for Beck to climb up there with her fear of heights. Knew she did that for Cassie.

Maybe it wasn't so unnecessary.

"Listen, I'm not going to call the cops. Just stop and go home now, okay?"

"Okay, boss," Beck said, laughing softly.

"Is this funny?" Vivian snapped. It was a long shift. EMT work beat the hell out of her, emotionally and physically. That's why she chose it. So she'd be too tired to think.

But tonight she just wanted to shower and sleep.

"Never thought I'd see the day you knowingly don't report my bad behavior."

"Well, congratulations. You get a free pass on account of my sheer exhaustion," Vivian said, turning away. "Go home, Beck."

Vivian climbed into her car and reached for the key. But the car was already on.

"No. No, no, no, no."

She prayed to every god she could think of for fifteen seconds, then tried the ignition again. Stalled. Totally, devastatingly, out of gas.

Vivian glared at her phone lying on the passenger seat. Like she had any kind of choice. She reached for it and opened her text messages. She scrolled for a while before realizing that what she was looking for didn't even exist.

There was no text exchange between her and Beck. Not on its own. It would have been a group chat with Cassie. She scrolled back up. The messages were still there. Dated the morning Cassie died.

Vivian called Beck instead.

"Change your mind? Calling the cops?" Beck asked instead of saying hello.

"My car died. Can I get a ride?"

"Shit, yeah. I'll pull around."

Vivian ended the call, and the screen lit up with the group text. The conversation she couldn't bring herself to get rid of, but couldn't bring herself to read again, either.

The last thing Cassie had sent was a SpongeBob meme.

CASSIE

It was always
the best part of my day—
riding to school with
Beck and Vivian.

Beck's angry music and
Vivian's angry eyes.
The two people
I loved most in this life,
barely tolerating each other,
but doing it anyway
for me.

Sometimes,
I could make them both
laugh at the same time.
I don't know why but

it felt like magic
and I felt most loved then.

So this is where I came
when I died:
to Beck's van.

BECK

BECK PULLED HER VAN ACROSS THE highway and let it idle behind Vivian's car.

When Vivian stepped out in front of the van's headlights, Beck saw her clearly for the first time tonight. For the first time in months. Vivian's brown hair was pulled into the same tight braids she had always worn to run track. Her eyes were tired and serious. She looked the same as ever, her thick brown eyebrows furrowed in deep thought, like she was overanalyzing every single thing she saw and heard.

Beck's hand slipped over the wide steering wheel, and she applied just enough pressure to chirp the horn. Vivian jumped, startled, then lifted her middle finger as she glared past the headlights.

Beck never could resist. Vivian had always been way too easy to rile.

Besides, this is how it used to be between them. How it would be still, if the universe made any damn sense at all.

Vivian climbed into the van, muttering a soft "Thanks for that."

"You're welcome," Beck said.

"Can we just get some gas so I can go home? We don't even have to talk," Vivian said.

Beck didn't answer, but she pulled off the side of the road and began to drive.

There was no connection for a phone to plug into. No Bluetooth in the old beast of a van, a classic VW bus that Beck's grandpa found in a decrepit—but cheap—state, and restored slowly over the years. When Beck was fourteen, he let her pick the color for its new paint job. She chose golden yellow. The color of the sunflowers. When he let her name it, she chose *Betty*.

Then on her sixteenth birthday, he surprised Beck by handing her the keys.

If anyone had told Tribeca Jones, age six and watching the stars for her salvation, that one day someone would lovingly restore a car just for the sake of her having something to drive . . . well, she'd have said keep the car and maybe put some food in the fridge or help her parents get sober, thanks.

Six-year-old Beck was possibly even angrier than teenage Beck. Practically feral.

But Beck loved the old VW bus more than she liked most humans and didn't care at all that the only music it played was the radio, and only when it felt like it.

Tonight when she twisted the dial, Betty offered them a sucker punch by playing one of Cassie's favorite songs.

"Shit," Beck said, reaching for the dial again, but Vivian blocked her hand.

"It's fine," she said, her voice low. "Let it go."

A minute passed . . . the music too upbeat for the way it was making them feel.

It was like Cassie was right there, a moment away instead of five months. For a second, Beck swore she could hear familiar humming. More than anything, Cassie had loved to sing. She was always singing in the back seat, humming along to the radio.

"The mural is beautiful," Vivian said out of nowhere, pulling Beck from the past.

Beck looked over, but Viv's eyes were down, watching her own hands twist in her lap. Whenever she got anxious, Vivian would rip all her nails off, like she was doing now. Beck reached over, her hand falling on Vivian's, stopping her.

"They shouldn't have left it up," Vivian said. "That was . . . I don't know. Cruel."

"No one cares if its cruel, Vivian. They care that Bell has jobs."

"I think it's more complicated than that," Vivian said.

"I don't," Beck said, her voice too sharp. It wasn't Vivian she was mad at. For once. Beck tried to soften her voice before she spoke again. "It's weird to listen without her."

"It's like I can hear her."

But Beck heard it, too.

Humming.

More distinct this time.

"Stop that, Beck." Vivian's voice broke on Beck's name, her anger biting through the word.

"I'm *not*. That would be fucked," Beck said. There were a million things she loved to torment Vivian about, but she would *never* about Cassie.

Beck slowed down on the highway, rolled to a stop on the shoulder to listen. If she was alone, she'd have blamed exhaustion. Isn't that what she'd done those other nights? When she thought she heard . . . something. Dismissed it as longing and grief.

The chorus hit.

A voice belted it—and the sound was coming from the back of the van.

They whirled in unison. At first Beck thought that she must have fallen off that billboard and hit her head so hard that she was either dead or unconscious. But Vivian was real and warm beside her after so many months. And this wasn't a dream.

In the back seat of the van, there was a faint outline in the darkness.

A shadow, in the shape of a girl.

Then it moved, climbing into the middle seat of the van.

26

The curve of her jaw was faintly there, but mostly not. The fall of her hair nothing but a wave of darkness.

But her eyes were the same bright blue.

The singing had stopped, and those eyes were fixed on them. They looked unnaturally wide with no face there to frame them. Only the soft, translucent shape of a familiar smile.

Cassie.

VIVIAN

VIVIAN HAD NEVER BEEN SCARED OF the monster under the bed.

She'd never believed in fairies. Not even the one sent to collect teeth. She'd chosen science over fiction, and truth over fable, from the time she was young enough to know the difference. Vivian didn't once scan the night sky for unidentified flying objects or lose sleep over a ghost story. Because ghost stories weren't real.

Except now she was in one.

Vivian reached across the van, her hand finding Beck's arm without taking her eyes off the back seat.

"Beck, do you . . . ?"

"Yeah, I see her."

"You do?" Cassie asked, climbing—floating?—into the middle seat of the van. Vivian could make out more details of her, but they were unfocused, there for a moment, then gone. Like her eyelashes on her cheek, and the dark indigo

28

of the denim jacket she was wearing when she died.

"What the hell is this?" Beck asked. She reached out, and Vivian drew in her breath, sharp, when Beck's hand passed through Cassie's barely there arm. "Why?"

"How?" Vivian asked.

"I don't know why," Cassie said. Her voice was the only thing unwavering about her. They heard her as though she was really right next to them. Which wasn't possible. "I don't know how. I've been here for a while and you couldn't see me, or hear me. Not until you two were . . ."

"Together," Vivian finished. Her hand was still on Beck's arm, like she needed to hold on to something—someone—to convince herself this was real, and not another one of the nightmares that had plagued her since March.

She squeezed her fingers together, pinching.

"Ow!" Beck yelled, pulling her arm away.

"Making sure it's not a dream," Vivian said, her eyes never leaving Cassie.

"That's not how that works," Beck said, rubbing her arm.

Cassie laughed.

And then Vivian didn't care *how* or *why*. She didn't want to question this at all. She just wanted to hear that laugh again. The one she'd missed every moment since March fifteenth, when it was stolen from her.

"I'm only here at night," Cassie said. "During the days, I'm too . . . wobbly. I'm nowhere. It's just me thinking then."

"I don't understand," Vivian said.

"Me neither," Cassie agreed. "Sorry if I scared you. You've never heard me before."

"I heard you humming," Beck said. "I just didn't think it was real. God, Cassie, we missed you."

Ghost Cassie turned to the window. There was nothing outside but acres of sunflowers.

"How's my family?" Cassie asked.

Broken to pieces, Vivian thought.

"They're . . . doing their best, Cassie," she said instead. "They moved away, back to your grandparents' town." It was true. It just wasn't the whole truth.

"Good," Cass said. "That's probably for the best."

Light pierced the still darkness of the van. The sun was rising.

"I'm gonna go away again," Cassie said. "See?"

She leaned forward, letting the shadow of her arm cross through the beam of light, where it disappeared. Before Vivian or Beck could protest, Cassie lifted her hand. "But I'll try to come back. Tonight. I think . . . I think maybe you both have to be here. I think maybe you are supposed to help me."

"Help with what?" Vivian was leaning toward the back of the van, hands clutched together, like she had to stop herself from reaching out and grabbing for Cassie to try to keep her there with them.

"What any ghost needs," Cassie said. "Closure."

"Closure?" Beck asked. The sun was warming the van, illuminating it too fast.

"Unfinished business," Cassie explained. "I've had a lot of time to think about this. I can't imagine why else I would be here. I just don't know what that *is*."

Vivian didn't know, either.

"It's vengeance," Beck said quietly.

Vivian whipped her head around.

"Just because your entire belief system is based on angry revenge fantasies doesn't mean the rest of the world is, Beck."

"Well, she has a point," Cassie said.

"Vengeance? Against who?" Vivian asked. "Nico is gone, Cass."

"Against Bell, I guess," she said, her shoulders lifting in a ghostly shrug. The gesture was so nonchalant, so *Cassie*. It was like she was a caricature of a ghost, not taking her haunting duties seriously enough. Yet here she was, dead—sort of—asking them to help her solve the impossible mystery of *why* she was here, so that she could move on for real.

A mystery to solve, a ghost, a van. And Beck probably had a stash of weed tucked under a seat. All they were missing was the dog.

"Which Bell? The town? The company? Mr. Bell?" Vivian asked.

"Yes," Beck answered.

"All of them," Cassie said as the sun rose over the tree line.

And as quickly as Cassie had returned to them, she was gone again.

WE CAN BE HEROES
SEASON 2: EPISODE 13
"THE SHERIFF"

MERIT LOGAN: Some background information. In March, seventeen-year-old Cassie Queen's ex-boyfriend, Nico Bell, brought his father's guns to school, shooting Cassie, one other classmate, and himself. The classmate survived. Nico and Cassie died at the scene. It could be argued that the small town of Bell is one of the most pro-gun places in the country, since it has been home to Bell Firearms since 1824, and the town was quite literally built around the company. A solid forty percent of jobs in town are held by Bell to this day. And Nico Bell was set to inherit the whole of it from his father, Steven Bell.

MERIT: I have a few more questions, Sheriff, about the events that led up to Cassie's murder.

SHERIFF THOMAS: Well, I'll try my best. But I can't say I know much. It was young love, gone terribly wrong. One of my officers handled the case. Wasn't high priority. Can't say why the kid did it. Why he thought that was the only way.

MERIT: The only way?

SHERIFF THOMAS: The only way to keep her. I don't know. Maybe he wasn't even planning to kill her. Maybe he just wanted to . . . to scare her.

MERIT: You think a seventeen-year-old took his father's guns to school to scare a girl he had previously acted violently toward?

SHERIFF THOMAS: I'm saying we don't know what was going on in his head. We couldn't have guessed his intentions.

MERIT: Sir, have you responded to domestic violence cases in the past?

SHERIFF THOMAS: Sadly, yes. We come across those cases rather frequently.

MERIT: How often? Just an estimate is fine.

SHERIFF THOMAS: About three a month in Bell.

MERIT: And how did Cassie's circumstances compare to those other calls?

SHERIFF THOMAS: This wasn't the same at all. They weren't adults. They weren't married or living together.

MERIT: So you didn't treat Cassie's case like you do other abuse cases?

SHERIFF THOMAS: There was no case, Ms. Logan. Nico Bell wasn't on our radar. They were *kids*. What kind of person expects kids to start killing each other?

MERIT: Maybe the kind of person whose job it is to be familiar with the dynamics of violence expects it. And they didn't *kill each other*, did they? *Nico* killed. Only Nico. You are talking about it like both of them are responsible. But let's move on, Sheriff. To the day it happened. Can you tell me what you remember of that morning?

SHERIFF THOMAS: It was a normal, quiet morning in March. We pride ourselves on that in Bell, you know. The low crime rates. No one robs a house in Bell. Or holds up the gas station. Because just about every single person is armed. Keeps the peace.

[Long pause]

MERIT: . . . Does it?

SHERIFF THOMAS: You know what I mean, Ms. Logan. It *did*. What are we going to do, take everyone's guns away just because one girl died?

CASSIE

At first death feels
like that time I almost drowned
in the lake
the summer we were twelve.

There wasn't pain, really.
Just an awareness that I
had gone under, an awareness
that soon I'd run out of oxygen.

Our rowboat sank
right in the middle
of the lake.
With me still in it.

I was trying to swim
back to the dock

but I overestimated
the distance, my strength.

And then there were
arms around me,
pulling me back to the surface,
getting me back to the dock.

The sun was high
and bright, right
behind his head,
forming a halo.

And when the paper wrote
about the incident,
a little block of text on page four,
they called him a local hero.

Nico.

BECK

BECK DIDN'T BOTHER TRYING TO SLEEP when she got home.

Instead she started the coffee and reached for Grandpa's pill bottles.

She counted them out, sorting them into a days-of-the-week container she'd picked up for him at the dollar store. It was mostly just pain meds, but the dosage was precise, so Beck counted and then counted again to make sure she had it right before tipping them into the plastic container.

Beck propped her phone up against a cup of orange juice, scanning the local paper online for some mention of—

There it was.

Vandalism on Route 90.

She didn't read the article, but locked her phone and tucked it in her pocket when she heard the familiar creak of the third stair from the bottom, just a moment before Grandpa stepped into the room.

He set his oxygen tank on the kitchen island across from Beck.

"Early morning?" he asked. "Or late night?"

Beck had stopped keeping secrets months ago.

"Late night," Beck told him.

Grandpa grunted, but the sound wasn't a chastisement. After Beck's mom, teenage rebellion in the form of staying out late to paint was an easy ride.

"Wear a mask?" he asked.

"Of course."

Grandpa left his coffee cooling on the counter and went to grab the paper from the porch. He kept it folded as he read, and Beck glanced up to see an inverted but familiar image.

Her mural.

On the front page of the paper.

"Shit," Beck said, earning a look of disapproval over the top of the paper.

"What?" Grandpa unfolded the paper, was quiet a moment as he read.

"Late night, indeed," he said, laying the newspaper down on the counter. "Anyone catch you up there?"

"No," Beck said automatically, then remembered the *no lying* promise they made to each other when Beck moved in. "Vivian."

"Ah," Grandpa said. "Maybe stick to some less-conspicuous locations in the future."

"But the sign had—"

"I know what the sign had on it. Which is why I'm not *scolding* you, Becks. Just imploring you to use some better judgment in the future. Don't get caught." Grandpa glanced down at the picture of the mural on the billboard. "It's beautiful, honey. God, I miss that girl."

Beck stared down into her cup at the sound of Grandpa's voice catching.

If Cass was like a sister to Beck, she had been like another granddaughter to him.

"Can you help in the garage today? Got a whole lineup coming in for oil, inspection, tires."

"No problem, Gramps," Beck said, downing the last sip of orange juice. "Okay if I take a quick nap?"

"First appointment is at ten; go sleep."

Upstairs, Beck crawled out of her stained overalls and into bed. She looked up at her ceiling, painted swirling navy blue and covered in stars. She'd wanted her room to look like the night sky.

She was just falling asleep when her cell began to ring. She glanced at the screen.

"Vivian, I'm trying to sleep," she answered.

"We should meet tonight," Vivian said. "In your van. Maybe if we're both there again, she'll come back."

"Okay, yeah. Sunset?"

"It's at eight thirty-two. Already looked it up, and . . ."

"And?" Beck asked, her eyes drifting shut as they talked.

"I've been thinking about what you said. About vengeance. I'm in."

Beck sat up in bed.

"You are?" She hadn't expected that from Vivian so quickly. Vivian usually made pro-and-con lists, debated endlessly. Considered a problem from every angle. And avoided getting in trouble at all costs.

Maybe Beck liked this new Vivian.

"Okay, well, shit. What are we gonna do? Burn the factory down?"

"God, Beck. *No.* We aren't burning anything down. You really aren't one for subtlety."

"No, I'm not."

Beck's phone started buzzing. It was Vivian wanting to video chat. When Beck answered she could see Vivian's bedroom, which looked mostly unchanged. The wall behind her was covered in shelves containing every annoying track trophy and spelling award and perfect attendance certificate that Vivian had ever gotten.

It was Vivian herself who had changed these last few months. She looked exhausted, and not just from their one late night with Cassie. The dark half-moons under her eyes looked like they had been made by months of sleeplessness. And Beck should know. Those same shadows greeted her in the mirror each morning, too. It was like Cass had been haunting them all this time, they just didn't know it until last night.

Vivian's hair was finally out of her tight braids, and she

had a mane of long, wavy brown hair framing her head.

Beck thought maybe she should say something nice to her.

"You look like a vampire," she blurted out. "But, like, the hot kind."

"Wow, gee, thanks, Beck."

Beck got out of bed and went to her window. The farmhouse had those old, deep well windows, and Beck curled up in one, folding her bare legs in front of her.

"We need to be strategic," Vivian said. Beck saw a notebook and pen on Vivian's bed, filled to the brim with her notes. She was *nonstop*. Even about this. "We need to go after Bell in the way that'll hurt them most."

"Meaning?"

"Their image," Vivian said. "Mr. Bell knew Nico was threatening Cass. The police knew it. No one did anything. They chose that company over her life. All we have to do is tell them what happened."

"Tell who?"

"Everyone. We have to tell everyone who will listen."

VIVIAN

THE VENGEANCE PLAN LOOKED LIKE THIS: six Xs on a map of Bell.

The locations were chosen carefully. Places they could work at night without being caught, but visible enough to warrant people's attention during the day. They wanted all of Bell to see them.

Vivian met Beck under the billboard just before sunset. Someone had to climb up to take a picture of the first mural, and Beck refused to go back up on that shaky platform a second time.

"Be careful!" Beck shouted from below while Vivian took the photos.

"I'm already done," Vivian called back as she climbed down the rusted ladder. When she reached the bottom, Beck was facing the other way, and Vivian tapped her shoulder.

"Couldn't watch you climbing around up there," Beck said.

Vivian didn't know all of Beck's secrets. They'd had

Cassie in common, but little else. Vivian was a good athlete, a great student, running as fast as she could toward her dreams. Beck preferred the quiet spaces. Being alone with her thoughts. She liked to paint and smoke and had always been more interested in fixing car engines with her grandpa than school. So Vivian didn't know *why* Beck was so scared of heights. But she knew Beck must have had a good reason.

She seemed to fear nothing else.

"Now what?" Beck asked.

"Now, a public service announcement." Vivian pulled up a new account log-in. She'd been thinking about this all day. Which platforms to use, and how to use them. They needed visuals. Somewhere they could post the mural and then photos of Cassie. They had to make everyone feel like they knew her, too. Like the loss was everyone's loss.

Vivian showed Beck her favorite photo of the billboard, adding it to a photo editor app to brighten the image and change the tones and colors. Vivian knew she wouldn't be the artist of this insane plan of theirs, but she could plan a social media campaign. She'd had enough practice on her own accounts, trying to project her own image of perfection.

She could be the architect behind their vengeance plan, right down to a perfect aesthetic.

"Tell me about the portrait," Vivian said, turning to Beck.

"It's Cassandra, from Greek mythology. Cassandra was a prophetess, but she was cursed. She could see the future, but no one believed her."

Vivian wrote the description under the photo, about the Greek myth. Added a title for the mural, simply *Cassandra*, and their location in Bell. Then she tagged a handful of gun-control advocacy organizations, and anything else she could think of to draw attention to Bell.

#dontforget

#bellgunskill

#justiceforcassie

"Okay, I'm posting it. Ready?" Vivian looked up to Beck for approval.

"Post it. Do it. Burn it all down, V."

Vivian rolled her eyes, looked back to the phone.

"Okay, our first Cassie mural is . . . up."

They sat staring at the photo on the phone, the little blurb of words underneath. Vivian had been confident about her plan, but now that it was up, it felt too small. It didn't seem like enough in the face of a mammoth like Bell.

The silence stretched between her and Beck. They weren't used to being alone together.

After the funeral, Vivian couldn't be around Beck at all. She was like a constant, sharp reminder that Cassie wasn't there. Only a Cassie-shaped space where she should have been, and it had felt like a black hole pulling everything toward it. Vivian couldn't avoid that feeling. So she avoided Beck instead.

She'd have gladly kept avoiding Beck forever if Cassie

hadn't come back to haunt them. "Did you know Cass was named for her?" Beck asked, interrupting the uneasy quiet between them. "Cassandra. That's why she always loved those Greek plays and stories so much."

"Remember the Halloween she made all of us dress up as goddesses, and you got to be Athena and have that fake sword and all the kids ran away from you?" Vivian asked.

"It was harmless, one of Cassie's theater props," Beck said, then smiled. "But it sure looked real."

"You got us all sent home."

"We went to Cassie's house, and we ate candy all afternoon. And then we were too sick to trick-or-treat. That was an awesome day."

"We got in so much trouble," Vivian said. It didn't matter if it was Halloween when they were twelve or parties when they were sixteen. Beck *always* got them in trouble.

"We had *fun*. Well, Cassie and I did. Maybe someday you'll figure out how to do it."

Their faces were suddenly cast in a shadow, distracting Vivian from whatever she was going to throw at Beck next.

"Beck. Sunset."

They both looked toward the van.

"Let's see if this works," Beck said.

While Beck drove, Vivian searched on her phone, finding the same song that was playing on the radio when Cass appeared the night before. They were like overzealous sports fans, convinced that some meaningless talisman worn on their body was the reason their favorite team won a big game. *It's superstition,* Vivian told herself. *You don't believe in these things.*

But tonight it didn't matter. She wasn't taking chances. Not if it meant they got to see Cassie again.

Beck parked the van on the same stretch of highway where she'd appeared last night. But none of it seemed necessary, because the moment the sky shifted from yellow to green-gray, they heard her.

"I'm here," she said softly, but she still sounded far away.

Vivian turned at the voice, her eyes finding the outlines of Cassie, still so faint but growing less translucent even as she watched. Cassie's denim jacket appeared, and tonight it was solid enough to see the button holes, and all of the little sunflowers that Beck had embroidered onto the back and edges of it for her as a birthday gift last year.

"Cassie," Vivian whispered, lost in awe all over again for a moment before collecting herself. They had work to do. "We have a plan. Beck, can you drive to the lake so we aren't just sitting on the side of the highway?"

Beck turned the van back on, shifting into gear and turning on the highway. Heading for Bell Lake. They'd spent every summer on the dock of the lake, stretched out in the ruthless sun until they couldn't take it anymore, then diving into the waters to cool off.

They'd gone to the lake when it was cold, too, in late fall and early spring.

It had started as retribution. Cassie forced Vivian and Beck to do a play with her their freshman year. Vivian *hated* it, and for once Beck seemed to agree with her. They were cast in the ensemble, and neither could sing. Beck couldn't follow a choreographed dance to save her life. But Cassie had insisted they stay in it so that they could spend more time together. High school had pulled them in different directions.

For Beck and Vivian, it was three months of extended humiliation that culminated when Beck knocked Vivian right off the stage at the curtain call of closing night.

After the show, they'd asked Grandpa to make a stop at the lake before going home, and Vivian and Beck had dragged Cassie down and thrown her off the dock before jumping in after her.

It had been late October, and the water was frigid.

But a tradition was born.

From then on, after every final performance Cassie was in, they all went and jumped in the lake, even if it was freezing.

"So this is what we are thinking," Beck said when she put the van in park. The lake looked dark and still, but the windows were rolled down, and Vivian could hear how alive the lake was in the summer—the frogs were peeping, and something was sloshing through the water. Beck reached for her sketchbook between the seats and opened it to show Cassie their map. "We have a vengeance bucket list. Six murals that I'll design and paint. Six locations around Bell. And a social media campaign to tell everyone the whole story of what happened to you. From the beginning."

Vivian opened her phone. The comments were already starting below her first post. Many of them were loving. Memories of Cassie from school friends. Condolences from strangers.

And then she found one from some guy that said: "That mural is vandalism. More crime is never the answer."

Vivian clicked through to his profile, and saw the man was from Bell, too. His photos were mostly of him posing awkwardly with his vast collection of guns.

Beck looked over her shoulder and scoffed. "You think maybe he's compensating for something?"

Vivian turned the screen toward Cass, who was hovering just over her shoulder in the middle seat of the van again.

"I know the type," Cassie said, and any other time, they might have laughed. But Nico wasn't someone they could laugh about anymore. "What makes you think people will actually care? They didn't before."

"I don't know," Vivian said. "Maybe they won't. But we have to show them *we care*. We haven't forgotten what happened. Something has to change so it doesn't happen again."

49

"You guys could get in a lot of trouble," Cassie warned. She said it to both of them, but she was looking at Vivian.

Vivian, the rule-follower.

Vivian, the straight-A student.

Vivian, who was bound for the best premed program in the country on a track scholarship.

But Cassie didn't know that the version of Vivian she had loved was gone—disappeared the day a bullet shattered a bone in her leg, stealing her ability to run track. The day a second bullet stole her best friend in a moment. And what could Vivian say? She had tried to get back to that place—to that *better* Vivian, but it was like trying to break into a stranger's mind and understand how they worked. *I don't know her anymore*, thought Vivian. *And I don't want to know her.*

"It's worth the risk," she told Cassie. "So you have to tell us everything. The parts we didn't know, too. And then we will tell the world your story. We'll make them listen."

"From the beginning?" Cassie asked.

"From the beginning," Vivian said.

CASSIE

It feels odd to call it
the night I met him
since we'd been together always,
in the same classes
since kindergarten.

But I remember the night
I met him.

Ethan Pine had been
stage director
for the fall production
of Beauty and the Beast.
His parents left town
so he threw a party.

We arrived soaking wet,
the three of us.

Lola Talbot pulled me aside
the moment we walked in.
Jesus Christ, Cass.
When are you guys gonna
stop jumping in the lake?
It's November. You'll
get sick and die and
then who
will play the spring lead?

I laughed at her then.
Because it was funny,
and because death felt so far away.
Neither of us could know
that in just sixteen months,
plus a few days,
Lola Talbot would watch me die
in our high school classroom.

But that night she said,
Nico is looking for you.
and I said, Bell?
which was such a stupid question
(which other Nico existed, or mattered?)
that Lola didn't answer me.

Lola did her very best
with what I gave her.
We'd changed into
dry clothes in the van,
but my hair was soaked.
You are pale and freezing,
like a corpse, *she scolded.*
She dragged me along the hallway
aiming for the bathroom,
where she was probably going to ring
the water from my mess of tangled curls
and put some lip gloss on me
but we didn't make it.
Nico Bell stepped in front of us,
blocking the hallway.

He said my name easily,
like we were already close.
Like he knew we would be.
Don't tell me
someone had to pull you
out of the lake
again?

His eyes were only on me,
and Lola squeezed my arm,

Good luck,
then disappeared.

I don't remember everything
Nico Bell said to me
that first night.
But I remember the way
his blond hair
fell into his face
while he talked.
He talked so much.
I thought he didn't mind
that I was quiet, shy.
But now I think
maybe he just
never cared
what I had to say.

He led me, winding
through the party,
tugging
me behind him,
his hand so warm
covering mine,
handed me a beer
as we passed the keg,
then outside to the fire.

There was only one chair left,
which he took,
gesturing
for me to sit on his lap,
which I did.
Then he took off his sweatshirt,
pulled it down over my head
and whispered in my ear:
Don't freeze on me, okay?
I don't want to be
the asshole responsible
for killing you.

WE CAN BE HEROES
SEASON 2: EPISODE 14
"THE FIREARMS EXPERT"

MERIT LOGAN: What happened to Cassandra Queen? If you ask the sheriff of Bell, it was young love gone awry—and Nico Bell wasn't an abusive killer, but a lovesick Romeo. Sheriff Thomas suggested that maybe Nico Bell didn't even intend to kill Cassie that day, only scare her. To talk about the likelihood of that idea, I've invited Olivia Ocasio to We Can Be Heroes. *Ms. Ocasio is a graduate of West Point. She served two tours in Afghanistan and is regarded widely as an elite markswoman and top firearms expert. She has testified before Congress on several occasions in relation to this expertise.*

MERIT: Thanks so much for joining me today, Ms. Ocasio.

OLIVIA: It's Olivia, please.

MERIT: Olivia. Thank you. Can we start with a description of the firearm that Nico Bell used in March at Bell High School?

OLIVIA: Of course. To start, he used two guns that day, which I haven't seen reported on very often. The first was a rifle, manufactured by Bell Firearms. It uses .223-caliber bullets. This is the kind of weapon that is usually referred to as an "assault rifle."

MERIT: What distinguishes that kind of rifle from others?

OLIVIA: Very little in the design. But this kind of rifle relies on extremely high velocity, and long, narrow bullets, to do what is it meant to do.

MERIT: And what's that?

OLIVIA: To wound beyond saving. The danger of these bullets is that they cause an enormous amount of internal damage on impact. You can talk to trauma surgeons who have seen this. The damage from these rifles isn't like a regular bullet wound, and CT scans highlight the difference really well. A regular bullet wound, like from a handgun, will show the trajectory of passage internally—a thin line. CT scans from rifle damage, like the weapon we are talking about, show widespread destruction—internal organs are essentially decimated by the force of impact.

MERIT: So are they more deadly than other weapons?

OLIVIA: More deadly than handguns, yes. Some other rifles are deadlier. But rifles like the one Nico chose are often used by mass killers because the bullets are cheap and lightweight. This is a question of access. Of who can get their hands on which weapons. Which is why I've testified in support of common-sense gun legislation. Not all guns are the same, and the law should reflect that.

MERIT: That's an interesting statement: *Not all guns are the same.* And it leads me to my next question. Can you talk about the second gun used that day?

OLIVIA: It was a Bell Firearm handgun. Nothing special,

except that it was very old. Probably taken from Steven Bell's personal collection. I think maybe it belonged to the founder of the company. It was valuable and rare. Likely one of personal and historical significance.

MERIT: Why *two* guns?

OLIVIA: The rifle would have been extremely deadly and accurate across the length of a classroom. Cassandra Queen was struck in the head and died instantly. But Nico, having grown up with guns, probably would have known that he could hit her anywhere on her upper body and she wasn't likely to survive it. The other classmate that was struck, however, was standing up. The bullet struck her leg. If it had hit her abdomen or chest, she very likely would have died, too. And then Nico dropped the rifle and shot himself with the handgun.

MERIT: With the handgun. The collectible.

OLIVIA: Correct.

MERIT: Okay, let's shift off that day. We understand what happened, and the weapons involved. We can draw a line and say that yes, Nico probably chose those two weapons intentionally, one for its deadliness and one for its personal significance. He wasn't planning on just scaring Cassie. He meant to kill her, and probably planned ahead of time to take his own life.

OLIVIA: I would agree.

MERIT: Okay, Olivia. I appreciate your candor here, so I'm

going to ask an odd question. Do you *like* guns?

OLIVIA: I've built my career on understanding guns. I believe in the Second Amendment. But no, I wouldn't say that I *like* guns.

MERIT: Can you explain that?

OLIVIA: Guns are a means to an end. In the military, that end is often violence against another human being. But in civilian hands? Without proper training, regulation, understanding of the weapon, and laws to keep those guns safely stored in the home, that turns into a practical free-for-all where citizens have access to any type of weapon they want. We're treating guns like toys. I've seen people argue that they should be able to have any gun they want just because they want it. There's no accountability in that. No respect for the weapon's deadliness when it inevitably falls into the wrong hands.

MERIT: But what about someone's right to defend themselves?

OLIVIA: Well, I think the more important question is, *whose* right? Because I can tell you that the gun lobbyists aren't speaking up when Black citizens with legally owned firearms are killed by police. They don't care about toddlers finding guns in the home and shooting themselves. Or women who are victims of intimate partner violence, held prisoners in their own homes because of the constant threat of a gun's presence. There's an enormous hole in the gun lobby's logic and it's the question of *who* is protected by a gun. If we have the right to a gun, don't we have the right to be kept safe from a gun, too?

MERIT: But can't women defend themselves *with* a firearm?

OLIVIA: Well, no. Cassie Queen couldn't. All she could do was say she was scared and ask for help. And many women who have defended themselves with a gun against an abuser have gone to jail for it. Every woman I served with in the military had their own firearm and expert training on how to use it. But look at statistics on assaults in the military. So the Second Amendment doesn't apply equally for everyone. Generally speaking, those refusing to talk about common-sense gun legislation are already an extremely privileged group of people.

MERIT: Does that group include people like the Bells?

OLIVIA: Exactly like the Bells.

MURAL 2

TITLE: ARIADNE

LOCATION: THE HIGH SCHOOL AUDITORIUM

BECK

AT JUST PAST ELEVEN THE NEXT night, Beck slipped out of her farmhouse, sneaking past her grandfather where he'd fallen asleep on the couch watching the news. She was careful not to wake him. She wouldn't know how to explain her plans.

Beck was on her way to meet a ghost. Again.

And to commit a crime. Again.

Beck rushed across the yard, eager to get to the van. Eager to reassure herself that the last two nights with Cassie weren't some strange trick of the universe.

But she didn't have to worry.

Cassie was there.

Beck could see her glow through the window before she even opened the door. Ghost Cassie was bluish all over. It was just a tint. Like moonlight was shining on her, except it was a new moon tonight, and the glow came from Cassie.

"Hey, Casper," Beck said, climbing in.

Cassie laughed, and Beck thought maybe she was more

solidly there tonight than last time. Beck could make out the individual waves of Cassie's long hair falling over her shoulders. The other nights it was just one dark mass.

"Casper," she said. "I like it."

"I have a surprise for you," Beck said. She pulled her phone out of her backpack and connected it to the little portable speaker that Vivian had left on the passenger seat. "It's new."

Beck pushed play on the album and watched Cassie's face as she realized what she was listening to.

"She dropped another album?" Cassie asked.

"Just a few weeks ago," Beck said.

"Oh my God!" Cassie shrieked. "We've spent two nights in this van and you didn't tell me?"

"We were a little preoccupied, Cass. With the whole . . . haunting thing."

"Unacceptable," Cassie said. "My otherworldliness doesn't trump new music from her."

"Well, I'm sorry that my priorities aren't as screwed up as yours. But I promise you can listen the whole time we paint."

"Right. Vengeance list. What does tonight's vigilante mural look like?"

Beck opened her sketchbook and turned it to Cassie.

"Wow," she said, reaching out to brush the page. She pulled back at the last moment, as though she remembered just then that she couldn't actually touch anything. "I always loved that myth."

"I know you did. Do. Sorry," Beck said. "This is weird."

"Yeah, it's weird," Cassie agreed.

They fell into a familiar quiet together, listening to Cassie's music until Beck pulled up to Vivian's house.

"Replay that last song again?" Cass asked, and Beck started it over again for her.

Vivian and her mom lived alone in a little townhouse. Her mom was a night-shift emergency room nurse, so Vivian had been alone overnight since she was twelve. Beck knew that she used to get scared. Instead of bothering her mom at work—they needed the money, and her mom couldn't afford to lose her job at the only hospital in the area—Vivian would text Cassie instead. And Cassie would text back as late as it took for Vivian to fall asleep.

Beck used to tease Vivian for it. Said she was scared of the dark.

As if Beck didn't know what it was like to hate being alone.

But Vivian was a perfectionist, which left very little to tease her about. Beck had to seize what opportunities presented themselves.

They'd decided to start this second mural around midnight. The location they'd chosen wasn't as visible as the billboard had been. They could start earlier, and with any luck not be seen.

Vivian's front door opened a moment after they parked. She must have been waiting by the door. Beck knew when

Vivian spotted that glow through the window. Her face lit with something joyous, a look full of so much love and longing, and Beck felt a pang of something at the sight.

She'd always been so busy torturing Vivian, she didn't imagine what it would feel like to make her happy. Vivian was the worrier, anxious, trying to be the best at absolutely everything. And she did it. She was so good at everything she did. Top of the class. Fastest on the track team. Fast enough to earn a track scholarship to the premed school of her choice. Vivian was what the high school guidance counselors called "driven."

And it had always annoyed the hell out of Beck.

Why kill yourself trying to meet everyone else's definition of perfect?

But tonight, when Vivian climbed into the van, she was genuinely smiling, despite her exhaustion.

And for once, Beck didn't feel like tormenting her.

"Hey, Beck. Hi, Cass. Like the music?"

"Of course I do," Cass said. "She's a lyrical genius. Beck, restart that last song again."

"You are, too," Vivian said, pressing skip to start the song over.

"Were," Cass said, switching tenses.

Cassie had always been writing music. And poems. She was particular with her language, using words to paint pictures the same way Beck did with acrylics.

Beck drove them to their destination, parking the van on the far side of the building just in case any rogue cars drove by tonight.

"I can't believe we are doing this," Vivian said, craning her neck to look through the front windshield at the wall they were about to paint.

"I can't believe *you* are doing this." Beck turned in her seat. "Okay, Casper, you've got your music. This should take us an hour or two."

"Casper?" Vivian asked. She was looking at the sketchbook.

"The friendly ghost," Beck explained.

Vivian could have leveled Beck with the look she gave her.

"Are you kidding? You can*not* call her that."

"Why not? She likes it," Beck said.

"It's funny," Cassie confirmed. "Not like *ha-ha* funny. But it's definitely funny in a *wow, how the hell did we get here* kind of way. You know?"

Beck smiled at Cassie casually joking about her own ghostliness, as only Cassie could, and then stuck her tongue out in Vivian's direction when she knew Cass was looking, making her laugh.

"I *don't* know," Vivian said. She turned, catching them making faces behind her back.

"Well, use your imagination. It's gotta be in there *some-where*," Cassie teased.

"Buried down deep," Beck said. "Under a memorized list

of every bone in the human body."

"We should get started," Vivian said, pivoting to the subject at hand and ignoring Beck's barb. She was all business, as usual, even when that business was a crime.

Beck had to admit, she was still surprised Vivian was even there.

She'd thought for sure Vivian would back out of this plan. She'd always been so obsessed with a clean record. Straight As. Perfect attendance. Anything that would give her the advantage to get into her dream school.

"Leave the windows down," Cassie said. "That way we can at least talk while you work, and you can listen to music with me. But first you have to restart that last song one more time."

"Cassie, we've listened to it three times already," Beck said.

"You can't say no to me. I'm dead."

"Well, I'm not restarting it. It's already seared into my brain."

Beck and Vivian left the windows open and started to work, pulling out the spray paint. Vivian began to group like colors together, and line them up in order of when they'd need them.

Beck rolled her eyes but let her do it.

Vivian propped the sketchbook open for Beck and was passing her the first can when they heard it. That song had restarted.

They ran back to the van, leaning through the open window.

Cassie was beaming, her finger hovering over the skip button on the music app.

"Did you just press that?" Beck asked.

"I did," Cassie said.

"You literally gained new ghostly powers just to listen to that song again?" Vivian asked.

"Sure did," Cassie said.

"Fine," Beck said, putting her hands up. "You earned it."

"Keep practicing," Vivian said. "Maybe you'll, like, be able to pick things up or something."

"Like what? I'm still stuck in the van. The best I could do is organize Beck's piles of clothes on the floor. They've been in here since March, by the way."

Vivian laughed. "Leave it. Unless you think your unfinished business in life is teaching Beck to be tidier. In which case, get used to being a ghost stuck in an old, smelly van, because you aren't going anywhere."

"Hey!" Beck said. "You *love* Betty. And this old, smelly van has been carting you two around town for years. Show her some respect."

"Betty is great. We love Betty *even when* she decides to not start in the dead of winter while we are freezing our asses off," Vivian said. "It's *your* mess we're critiquing."

Vivian and Beck moved around the van, pulling out the

stepladder they needed to reach the higher parts of the wall. It was a large design. They had coverage on almost all sides, and it was summer, so no one would be around. But it was still a risk.

"Imagine if we could go back in time and tell Past Vivian she'd be helping me destroy school property," Beck said.

"Well," Vivian said, handing Beck her next paint can. "Depends on how far back you go. I think any version of me from March onward would surprise you."

"You're right. I thought you'd be distracted with getting ready to leave for college."

"I'm not," Vivian said.

"Not distracted?" Beck asked, tugging her mask into place. Tonight, she was painting a maze, and she had to focus to make straight long lines on the side of the building. They had chosen the wall outside the auditorium, where Cassie had taken the stage so many times.

"Not going," Vivian answered.

Beck stopped painting. Vivian wasn't going to college? She'd dreamed of that admittance letter since they were kids. Vivian had always wanted to be a doctor. And she'd gotten into the premed program of her choice.

"Do you want to talk about it?" Beck asked.

"Nothing to talk about," Vivian said. "Can't run anymore. So, no more track scholarship."

Beck pulled the paint can trigger again. She tried to focus

on the lines—the design was more complicated, and she didn't want to make a mistake.

But she couldn't leave it alone.

"You've wanted that school since we were nine," Beck said.

Beck remembered, because it used to make Beck feel a warm prickle of jealousy whenever the subject came up. Vivian always had those big dreams, and she never once apologized for it or tried to make them seem smaller than they were.

Beck could barely move beyond the survival mode she'd been stuck in.

"Things changed," Vivian said.

"That's not good enough," Beck said, whirling on the ladder to face her. Each of them had a mask in place to shield them from the paint fumes, and all Beck could see of Vivian were her eyes. Illuminated only by the van's far-off headlights, they were dark and wild and angry. Beck recognized the warning in them. The one that said *Don't corner me or I'll bite.* But Beck knew a wounded creature when she saw one. It was like looking in a mirror.

"You have to go," Beck said. "You can borrow money and apply for grants. Did you even talk to the school—"

"Stop it," Vivian said. "I've already decided, weeks ago. It doesn't feel right anymore."

"But, Vivian—" Beck said.

"*Enough*, Beck," Vivian said. "If I can let it go, you can, too. I'm going to stay here with my mom, and you aren't going to change my—for the love of God, Cassie!" Vivian turned and shouted over her shoulder at the van. "*Please move on to the next song.*"

Cassie started the same one over again.

"You know she has to get it out of her system," Beck said. "Remember when it was that one Adele song for six weeks?"

"Oh my God, I had that song stuck in my head for months. My dreams had that song in them."

"My grandpa knew the lyrics because I sang it under my breath so much."

"Aww, poor Grandpa." Vivian laughed.

"He never minded anything Cassie did," Beck said.

"Or any of us," Vivian said. "He's a saint. A grumpy mechanic saint."

"True."

Beck spray-painted a figure in one corner of the maze. A girl. She was small, trapped in a thicket of twists and turns. And in the center of the maze, Beck made the monster. The Minotaur, tall and beastly, searching for the girl.

Beck painted one last line, sealing them in together.

The maze had no way out.

She'd been left in there on purpose, as bait. A meal. Something to appease the creature so it didn't question the walls built around it. Cassie was always interested in Greek myths, and this one had been special to her, but even more so in the last year. Something about being lost, and stuck, had resonated with Cassie.

Of course, it made sense to Beck now. If only she'd realized sooner. Cassie didn't have the words to ask for help. So she told stories. It had been Cassie trapped all along. And there were no bread crumbs or strings to show her the way out.

It took another half hour of touch-ups before she was satisfied with the mural, climbing off the ladder and tugging down her mask.

She stood back from the wall with Vivian, looking up at the maze.

"It's amazing," Vivian said. "We'll have to swing by in the daylight to get a good photo of it."

"That's fine," Beck said. "We'll be careful."

"What should I call this one?" Vivian asked.

"Just the name again," Beck said. *"Ariadne."*

"Can I tell you a secret?" Vivian asked, leaning closer to Beck.

"Of course," Beck said, matching Vivian's whisper.

"I really wish Cassie couldn't push that damn button."

Beck stood in the doorway of her grandfather's room.

It was just past three in the morning, and Beck was sneaking back in.

Checking on him at night had become a habit of hers since his diagnosis. She'd slip into his room anytime she awoke in the night, sometimes in a panic, the fear waking her, convincing her he was already gone.

Now it was almost inevitable, nearly every night, that panic. At least tonight she'd skipped the waking part and could collapse in her bed after checking on him.

It was the same way he used to check on her when she first came to live here.

It was like in the shop. The sicker he got, the more work she took on. It was a role reversal, slow and steady. From care receiver to caregiver. Grandpa didn't know that Beck knew he used to check on her every night, too. He'd stand there in her doorway for a moment, making sure she was still there. Making sure she hadn't slipped away in the dead of the night the same way her mother used to do, chasing parties and Beck's dad. Chasing that forever until it killed them in a drunken car wreck, and Beck was sent to live with a grandfather she'd never met.

He hadn't even known Beck existed until the authorities called him. And then they became each other's whole world. But now he was sick. Now it was Beck who worried about someone leaving.

The doorway wasn't close enough, so Beck walked over to the bed, laid her hand gently on his back. She waited until he drew a few deep breaths before retreating.

Beck opened her bedroom window. She would have texted Vivian, to figure out a time, early, to go get a good photo of the mural for their social media posts, but her phone was out in the van, playing Cassie's new favorite song on repeat.

It could wait. The paper might even cover this mural, too, and give them a photo to use.

Beck curled up in the deep-set window seat in her bedroom, tugging an old throw blanket over her bare legs. She could hear Cassie's music, faintly, from where Betty was parked next to the sunflower field that ran right up to the edge of Grandpa's property.

It was a pretty song, Beck had to admit.

She fell asleep listening to it, knowing that Cassie was out there, listening, too.

CASSIE

Ariadne memorized
the Minotaur's labyrinth.
She learned the steps
and then followed her feet,
through the darkness
to safety.

Then she taught the others,
and saved them, too.

Philosophers call it
Ariadne's thread.
It means you have exhausted
all your options
to figure out a problem.
It means trying
each and every logical path,
keeping track

of your failures,
until you find the answer.
It means
you are deliberate
in the way you
seek a solution.
Like how my friends
are being deliberate,
sure-footed,
in how they help me.

In poems, Ariadne is
the softhearted one,
as though saving lives
is some kind of weakness
or fatal flaw.

But I think maybe Ariadne
understood survival
in a primal way.
Knew that if she lost track
for one moment in that maze,
she would be lost to it, too.

I spend a whole day thinking
about liminal spaces.
A liminal space could be

a train,
or a bridge,
an elevator,
an airport,
a bus,
or the bus terminal.

They are the in-between,
the road and the journey,
but not the destination.
A space you occupy only
temporarily.

I think of the wings
of the stage, dark
and full of whispers,
where we still felt that distance
from the audience.

I remember the moment
right before I stepped out,
the moment I thought,
What the hell am I doing?
What if it all goes wrong?
But then I followed my feet
in the darkness,

took that last step
despite all of that fear,
and out in the lights
my whole world
transformed,
and so did I.

Onstage,
I was somehow
more of myself.
Onstage,
I found my voice.

It's strange, the things I miss.
Little details of my life
I barely even noticed
but now yearn for:
the feeling of the summer
sun on my shoulders.
Breathing in the scent of
sunflowers in July,
those stage wings and
the whispers of friends.

I think maybe the labyrinth
was a liminal space, too.

Ariadne leading lost ones
through the darkness, safe
as long as she remembered
to follow her feet.

And I wonder if maybe now
I am a liminal space, too.

There is something wild
and vulnerable about a
temporary existence.

And there is something
wild and vulnerable
and, of course, temporary
about me.

VIVIAN

VIVIAN WOKE TO A HAND ON her shoulder, gently shaking her awake.

"V. V, wake up."

She opened her eyes to find a concerned Matteo. His curly brown hair was falling into his face as he leaned over her. Vivian panicked and sat up fast, cracking her head against his with the movement.

"Shit," she said, hands flying up. She placed one on her own head and the other found Matteo's bruised skull. "I'm sorry."

Then she realized where she was. In the ambulance, on a shift. She fell asleep on the ride back to the station from the hospital. Dammit.

"I'm so sorry, Matteo. I swear that won't happen again." Vivian reached for her coffee, gone bitter and cold, but it would still do the trick to wake her up a little more. It had been a long night, first painting with Beck, and then they'd stayed out even later just to spend all the time they could with Cassie.

Now it was only 4:30 p.m. and she was passing out on her shift.

"It's no problem, V. But are you okay? You called off a shift, and you're falling asleep the moment you stop moving." Matteo's words didn't sound annoyed so much as concerned. Like Vivian calling off work and falling asleep wasn't impacting him—even though she knew it was. "You look exhausted. Like fucking *wiped*. Pale and sad. Like a vamp—"

"If one more person compares me to a vampire, I'll scream," Vivian warned, and Matteo snapped his mouth shut.

Matteo parked the ambulance and Vivian didn't wait even a second before swinging open the door and climbing out. If Vivian knew anything, it was how to run. Besides, Vivian didn't have a good excuse for Matteo to explain how tired she was, and her brain was too tired to make something up on the spot.

Oh yeah, well, my best friend who was the victim of a school shooting—remember Cassie?—well, she's back as a ghost and we're working on a vengeance plan to help her find closure and move on, only that plan is fundamentally based on vandalism and public shaming of the multibillion-dollar company that controls this town.

Vivian stopped just short of running into Matteo. He had

circled the other side of the ambulance, meeting her around the back. He placed a hand on her shoulder and waited for her to meet his eyes.

"Hey, V. It's me. I'm not going to hound you. I'll just say this: I'm here for whatever you need. I know . . . I know how much you're hurting. I miss her, too."

Matteo had always been a good friend.

Which made it harder to lie to him.

"I'm just not sleeping well," Vivian offered instead. A lie by omission. She was getting good at those. "But I'm fine." Big lie. "It's just nightmares, and I've been assured they'll fade with time." So many lies.

Matteo and Vivian had grown up together in a lot of ways. Their mothers were good friends—both single moms, and they helped each other out, sending Matteo and Vivian back and forth down the block of row homes they both lived in. They'd shared birthday parties, rides to school, even their grandmothers. They both wanted to be doctors.

They had so much in common. Until now. Because Matteo was still planning on leaving for college in six weeks, and Vivian wasn't.

And because Matteo's mom worked for Bell Firearms. Vivian didn't know how to talk to him about that, either. He hadn't been there in that room when it happened. And he could say he understood, but he didn't. No one did.

It wasn't like Vivian hadn't tried. She had gone back for

her final exams. They'd set up a Saturday in May for her and the other seniors who had been in the room that day. Six of them. They had been allowed to finish their classes from home, but they had to do exams in person.

The moment Vivian had sat down at that desk, her hands began to shake. She couldn't stop glancing at the door, waiting for chaos to strike. Her brain knew logically that she was safe, but her body didn't.

She panicked. And left.

And it didn't matter to her, when Principal Ewing had reached out to her, saying that they were passing her anyway. That she was graduating with her class. That she would keep the title she'd worked so hard for: valedictorian.

It didn't matter because Vivian didn't know how to sit in a classroom anymore. Didn't trust herself not to panic again. She wasn't the same person as before. The one who tried hard. Who decorated her room with awards and trophies and track medals, like those things mattered. The one who had all of her dreams right at her fingertips—all of the hard work and planning she and her mom had put into her future. The one who had two best friends to lean on.

The things that had once meant everything to Vivian meant nothing now.

Vivian pulled out her phone after saying goodbye to Matteo—she had a stream of messages from Beck.

Check the account.

Look at the numbers.

Vivian logged in to the social media account she had made for the murals.

Her fingers froze over the screen. It was working.

"Cassandra" had hundreds of comments. It had been shared by an organization advocating gun control. By a podcast about violence against women. By a congresswoman.

The numbers were climbing as she watched.

For the first time in a while, Vivian felt that little thrill of anticipation. The one she always felt when she'd done something she set out to do. That feeling of overcoming the odds. Of winning the race.

It felt like she was setting the world on fire, making it burn with all the hurt that she had locked away inside of herself. It was the only thing shaping her anymore. The only thing that was now bringing her back to herself after being trapped for so long. Finally, Vivian felt a flicker of recognition. For that part of herself that was new and foreign, the part she hadn't been able to accept or understand, so it had frozen her in place for these long months.

Vivian had thought it was grief, that feeling that had consumed her all this time.

But she'd been wrong.

It was rage.

BECK

BECK HAD THREE HOMES IN THE town of Bell.

Her grandpa's farmhouse.

The barn where he ran his mechanic shop.

And the art supplies store on Main Street in town.

Beck had been sneaking art supplies before she found it. A tube of paint from the art classroom. A paintbrush from her teacher's desk. But then she got caught, and Grandpa took her to the art store. From then on, all of her birthday wish lists had been canvases, watercolors, oil pastels.

Beck had never been religious, and though her grandpa attended church every Sunday, he said it was because it had been important to Beck's grandma, so it made him feel closer to her. Beck understood that, because painting made her feel close to her lost mother, too.

The art supplies store was the closest thing to a church—a sanctuary—that Beck had known. She could spend hours inside, examining bristles and testing out new paints. She'd been friendly with the owner, Ruth, for years, on a first-name basis since Beck was just thirteen. Beck got along better with adults than kids her own age. Her therapist had told her that was common in kids who experience neglect or trauma. *Your brain had to be wired like an adult,* she'd told her. *You became the caretaker.*

Not a very good one, Beck had thought at the time.

Beck parked Betty on a side street, tucked away from the storefront. They had just swung by the high school for a few photos of their mural, and Vivian was busy as ever, posting the next mural on social media.

"How's that going?" Beck asked, leaning over. "Wow. Shit."

Vivian had the first mural post up, checking its progress. It had a thousand comments. And over five thousand likes.

"It's going . . . really well," Vivian said. "These comments were all Bell residents at first. A lot from friends at school. But it's spreading. The gun control groups I tagged shared it, too."

"So . . . it's working."

"I think so?" Vivian shrugged. "People are talking about Cassie. About Bell. Listen to this." Vivian pulled the headphones out of her phone and hit play.

". . . series on gun violence, focusing on the town of Bell, and the school shooting that occurred there last year. Like so many incidents of public and mass shootings, this one was driven by an abusive relationship. It's a facet of

87

violence we don't dig into enough."

Vivian hit pause.

"What is that?" Beck asked.

"A podcast. It's called *We Can Be Heroes*, and it's about violence against women. Listen to this description. *'Every week I interview survivors of violence, harassment, and assault. Our guests are welcome to remain anonymous, or not. And they are invited to name names, or not. Always at their discretion. This is a show that, in its infancy, was called a "libel lawsuit waiting to happen"—but last week was heralded by the* Times *as a "revolution against gender-based violence" when our podcast hit a milestone of twenty-five thousand downloads per episode.'*"

"And she's talking about Bell?"

"She's *in* Bell. She interviewed the sheriff about Cassie."

"And?"

"And he's an ass. We knew that. But this podcast has a huge audience. Last year it got some bank CEO arrested for harassing his assistant, all because of an interview she did. She's literally out to take these guys down. And she shared *our mural post* with her followers."

"Feels weird to have someone on our side," said Beck.

"Yeah, it does."

"Okay, I'm going in. It's hot today, so I'll leave Betty running, for the air." Beck didn't add the other reason she wanted the van on. In case they needed to get away fast. Beck didn't think the police were really concerned *yet*. But they would be soon. And they'd be looking for anyone buying a shit ton of paint.

"Mm-hmm," Vivian murmured from the passenger seat. She had a notebook in front of her and was writing furiously. "Based on how much paint you used for the first mural and for the maze, we will need . . . at least twelve for the next one."

"Okay. You have the color list?"

Vivian flipped her notebook, pulled off a sticky note, and handed it over.

Five colors and their serial numbers were listed. And the aisle and shelf.

"Jesus, Vivian. This isn't a school project," Beck said, but there was no bite in her teasing. Secretly, it made Beck feel better, to see a little bit of the old Vivian shining through. The version of her that was excited and driven and always had a project or a plan or some other annoying thing going on. Then Cassie died, and that version of Vivian disappeared; Beck couldn't even be around her. She felt like she didn't know the new Vivian, who was withdrawn, exhausted, aimless. But today Beck could see glimpses of that old Vivian again. Only now she was motivated almost exclusively by anger.

Welcome to the club, thought Beck.

The anger had been there for Beck all along, like water running over her, again and again, eroding her, shaping her into something new all the time.

This was new to Vivian, being shaped by anger. It was

89

easy to let it take over everything.

"You okay?" Beck asked, standing at her open driver's side door, watching Vivian type away on her phone, getting ready to post the *Ariadne* mural on their account.

"Great," Vivian said, not looking up.

Beck rolled her eyes and shut the door. The sun was starting to set—Cassie would probably be there by the time Beck got back.

She hurried into the store, waved to Ruth behind the counter.

"Beck, honey, can I help you find something?"

Ruth had been a bona-fide hippie in the '60s, and you could still tell that there was something wild about her even now. She left her gray hair to grow and wore it long and loose around her shoulders. She was always brushing a hand through it and leaving some paint behind. She often painted behind the counter while she waited for customers. When she called out to Beck, she didn't even look up from her canvas.

"No!" Beck called as she turned down an aisle. "Thank you, Ruth."

"You here for more paint, honey? Are you finally covering that big wall of your grandpa's barn?"

"Yeah, finally," Beck said. Her heart rate ticked up.

Ruth had already noticed her buying more spray paint than usual.

"Oh, Beck, don't forget to check those new brushes that came in."

"Thank you, I see them," Beck said. "They're beautiful. But I'm broke, Ruth. I get paid Thursday. I'll be back for them."

She tried to take her time, browsing like she always did. Rushing in and out in five minutes would be even more suspicious. Eventually she made her way to the spray cans, checked Vivian's list, and pulled the paint canisters off the shelf.

It was fine. Beck was always painting. This wasn't that unusual.

The bell over the door rang as Beck turned the corner. She was walking back up to the register and stopped short.

There was a Bell police officer *right there*, talking to Ruth.

". . . murals popping up. Thought it was a fluke, a one-time thing. But we just found another. Has anyone been buying up a ton of paint suddenly? It's a small town. You're the only art supplies store."

Ruth didn't look at Beck. But she must have known that Beck was standing there, arms full of cans of paint.

"I haven't noticed anything unusual," Ruth answered.

Beck ducked back into the paint aisle.

She hurriedly put the cans down and made her way back to the front of the shop.

"Bye, Ruth!" she called out, like she always did. Trying to

not look like she was running even though the urge was there.

"Beck, dear. Your pre-order came in," Ruth said. "If you head around to the back door, I'll bring the box out of my office for you."

"My pre-order?" Beck asked.

"Just head around back. I'll be there in a minute."

Beck didn't understand, but she circled around the building anyway. She stood there and waited, her eyes finding the security camera fixed on the wall outside.

A minute later, Ruth popped open the back door of the shop that led into an alleyway. She held out a box for Beck.

"Give them hell, honey," was all she said, and let the door swing shut again.

Beck opened the box. All the paint cans she'd been holding were in there, plus some extra ones. Ruth had also dropped in a set of those fancy brushes. She had all the paint she needed, without so much as a credit card receipt linking her to it.

Beck would send Ruth cash for the supplies. And she'd paint something just for her, as a thank you.

When Beck came back around the shop, the police were still out front.

Beck kept moving, willing herself not to hurry, until she climbed back into the van parked down the street.

"Hey," Cassie said from her now-usual spot in the middle seat.

She was lying down across it. Beck could make out all of Cassie's individual curls of hair tonight, though the wispy ends turned invisible before they reached the floor of the van.

Probably better, since that floor was covered in T-shirts and empty paint cans and trash.

"That go okay?" Vivian asked, and frowned at Beck's face. "You weren't acting conspicuous, were you? I knew I should have gone in."

"It was fine," Beck said, dropping the box between the seats and starting to drive. "No big deal."

Cassie sat up a bit.

"You *sure* you're okay?" Cassie asked, leaning forward, studying Beck's profile.

"Yes, why?" Beck snapped.

"Because you look like you've seen a ghost," Cassie said, and for a second she held the serious look on her face.

Then Vivian snorted from the passenger seat, and the two of them burst out laughing.

When Beck first moved in with her grandfather, she was eight years old and obsessed with death—much to the horror of her third-grade teacher and the parents of the few friends she had made and just as quickly lost. The only people who didn't mind her morbid preoccupation with mortality were Cassie and Grandpa.

Beck was searching for answers, and there were none to be

found. So instead she clawed her way through every idea of the afterlife she could find, scouring religions from ancient times until now for a better understanding. But somehow Grandpa understood what Beck was looking for. She wanted to know *where* her mother was, if not there with her.

When she first came to live with him, Beck never left the shop while Grandpa worked. She liked to be where he was all the time. She would hand him tools when he asked for them, and he'd ask her to repeat the correct names of them. And she would sit at his workbench and draw dead things.

When Beck drew dead things in school, they would call Grandpa. But when she drew them at home, he never told her to stop.

"Heaven isn't for perfection, Beck," Grandpa said one day, not looking up from his work under the hood of the car.

Beck remembered her mom's soft blond hair. Her skin was so fair it was almost translucent, and Beck could follow the veins up and down her arms. Blue road maps that didn't frighten Beck, because she knew they meant her mom was alive. Her mother wasn't perfect, but she was human, and she tried. She tried to stop drinking.

But Beck didn't know if that was enough for heaven.

"Why isn't heaven for perfect?" Grandpa asked that day.

Beck had shrugged. "I dunno."

The hood of the car slammed down, and Grandpa was

looking at Beck. "Because nobody is perfect, Beck. Nobody. And if heaven was for perfect it would be empty. If you ever meet a person who acts like they think they're perfect, well, you've probably just met the biggest sinner of us all."

He shuffled over to the workbench and studied Beck's drawing, a bird lying on its back, eyes open and unseeing. He didn't comment on it.

"It isn't for the perfect. It's for the repentant. It's for the people who say 'I'm not always good, but I'm trying. I'm sorry for my mistakes. I repent.'"

And that was it. The magic word that eight-year-old Beck had needed to hear.

Trying.

Because Beck knew her mom had tried as hard as anyone ever had.

After that, Beck's obsession with death faded away. She had a best friend. Two, if you counted Vivian. A stable home. Security. But every night before she went to bed, even long after she stopped believing in heaven and everything else, Beck would whisper fiercely, "I repent. I repent."

When Beck got home from their art supplies run, she laid out the new brushes and the cans of precious paint that they needed to keep making murals for Cassie. All of it had been handed over to her on a system of trust. Someone showing her a bit of grace when she needed it the most. And the memory of that day in the barn with

Grandpa and those words came back to her again.

I repent. I repent.

Beck just wanted the universe to know.

This was her trying.

WE CAN BE HEROES
SEASON 2: EPISODE 15
"THE DEPUTY"

MERIT LOGAN: Before we get into the issues, a bit of breaking news. Earlier today, a second mural of Cassie Queen was discovered in the town of Bell, this time on the side of the high school auditorium, depicting another Greek legend—Ariadne and the Minotaur, trapped in the labyrinth.

What's interesting about these murals, other than the way they are mysteriously appearing overnight in the small town, is the social media account that is posting photos of the murals, all in Cassie Queen's name. Listen to this caption from the second mural:

"Cassie was trapped in a labyrinth, too. And Nico Bell was in there, stalking her. Cassie was scared. She knew Nico was dangerous, and she tried to get help. But the system wasn't built to keep Cassie safe. It was built to protect Nico from the accusation—God forbid we hold abusers accountable for their actions. Who else knew Cassie was in danger? Who do you think, @BellPoliceOfficial and @BellFirearms? #CassieKnew #TheyAllKnew."

You can find a link to it in today's show notes. Sheriff Thomas wasn't able to join us again, so today we've asked one of his deputies, Officer Daniel Everett, to talk to us about this strange pattern of—What do we even call this? Vigilante art?—emerging in the town of Bell this last week.

MERIT: Officer Everett, I'm so glad you could make it today.

EVERETT: Well, Sheriff Thomas asked me to hop on to this call and clear up what seemed to be some . . . misunderstandings you had last time. We value transparency in Bell and want to set the record straight.

MERIT: I appreciate that. So let's dive in. Bell has been the site of some controversial vandalism this last week. What can you tell us about the murals?

EVERETT: Not too much beyond what the *Bell Review* has printed so far. This is an open investigation. But I can say we have a pretty good idea we are looking for some local kids.

MERIT: Why do you think that?

EVERETT: Looking at the social media posts, this is a very specific, aimed message. The posts include tags for local places where teens hang out, like the Loft, a café in town, and the high school itself. It seems they want that message to reach teens directly in addition to some big gun control organizations. And the language is worded in a way that feels juvenile.

MERIT: What makes you think that the muralists are the same people posting to the media accounts? Isn't it possible someone is painting and someone else is taking these photographs and posting online?

EVERETT: Well, we've found—hang on a sec.

[Indistinct shuffling sounds]

EVERETT: Sorry, ma'am, no comment.

MERIT: Can you confirm if you have any suspects at this time?

EVERETT: . . . No comment.

MERIT: You know what? Let's move on to something else. Officer Everett, I have a copy here of Cassie Queen's request for a protection order, filed on March thirteenth of this year.

EVERETT: I believe Sheriff Thomas filed that request.

MERIT: That's right. Is it typical for the sheriff himself to fill out paperwork like this? Requests for protection orders?

EVERETT: Not sure if it's typical, but I know he made a point to go see Cassie Queen in the hospital that day.

MERIT: It seems he did. I have a question about the form. There is a box here that needs to be checked to request that any firearms are removed from the abuser's home.

EVERETT: A judge needs to make that determination; it's just a request. The judge has to decide if there is enough indication of a threat to temporarily surrender firearms for a temporary protection order—at least until a formal hearing takes place. A judge can only order someone to permanently surrender all their firearms in a final protection order.

MERIT: But the box wasn't even checked on Cassie's form. Do you know why this wasn't requested?

EVERETT: No, ma'am, I do not. And like I said, it wasn't my paperwork.

MERIT: I actually went ahead and pulled the last fifty requests for protection orders in the county. Nineteen of those requests were from Bell. Do you want to guess how many of these requests for temporary protection orders—again, just for the interim time it takes to schedule a formal hearing and secure a permanent protection order—do you want to guess how many of those fifty requests have that box checked?

EVERETT: I really can't say.

MERIT: All of them. All fifty. Including the nineteen from Bell. Except for Cassie's.

EVERETT: Well, you'll have to ask the sheriff about the form.

MERIT: I had planned to. But he changed our interview last-minute. I'm just wondering why Cassie's case against Nico Bell was treated any differently from other cases. The sheriff himself went to the hospital. Filed the form. Didn't check that box.

EVERETT: And I can't comment on that.

MERIT: Officer Everett, you said you were here because you value transparency. Is there anything you can comment on about this case?

EVERETT: No. But I would like to say something to the vandals, if that's all right by you.

MERIT: So you can't answer my questions, but you want

to use my platform to get a message out?

EVERETT: Ms. Logan, I don't know about where you're from—

MERIT: Actually, I grew up in—

EVERETT: —but we take property destruction extremely seriously in Bell—

MERIT: —as opposed to the violence that Cassie Queen experienced—

EVERETT: —and they ought to know we won't stop until we have someone to hold responsible.

MERIT: —at the hands of her ex-boyfriend, Nico Bell. You didn't take that *extremely seriously*, did you? Who do we hold responsible for that?

EVERETT: I don't like what you're implying, Ms. Logan.

MERIT: I'm not implying anything, Officer Everett. I'm outright saying it. You let Cassie Queen slip between the cracks, and I'm trying to find out what happened. Now you are putting all your efforts into tracking down a couple of teens trying to honor her memory.

EVERETT: From where I'm sitting, they just want to create division. They're criminals.

MERIT: Was Nico Bell a criminal?

EVERETT: Not until he pulled that trigger.

MERIT: Don't you think something could have been done before that—

EVERETT: Ms. Logan, we can stop some criminals *right*

now if you'd let me talk. The last thing this town needs is more chaos, divisiveness—

MERIT: I think the word you are looking for is justice.

EVERETT: And I think this interview is over, Ms. Logan.

VIVIAN

VIVIAN HAD ALWAYS LOVED MAPS. SHE'D asked for a globe for her fourth birthday. She used to spin it, put a finger on it, and then she and her mom would look up that place together. They'd imagine traveling there one day. When she decided she wanted to be a doctor, she'd gotten a world map for her wall. She researched organizations that sent doctors all over the world. Doing real good. Changing people's lives.

Vivian wanted that future, and the moment she'd decided on it, there had been nothing else for her. She used pins, marking the places she'd want to travel one day to work. After Cassie died, she took that map down. She'd left the wall blank, empty. She didn't have anything that she wanted in its place.

Until now.

Now Vivian put up a new map. One of Bell. They didn't actually sell maps of Bell, so she'd asked Beck to make one for her, to track their vengeance plan, to see all of the places they were putting the murals. It was her new obsession.

There was a winding gray line that ran off the side of the page—Route 90. And a little square where the billboard stood. Vivian scribbled a little heart under it on the map and filled in the number of likes that mural now had online: 8,998.

Almost nine thousand people, more than the entire population of Bell, reading Cassie's name. Learning her story. Agreeing that something more must be done.

And then she added the second mural. An X marks the spot, this time on the western side of the high school, where a block of red showed where the auditorium was. Beck said they'd found it. It was good she'd swung by after her shift to get a good photo of the mural in the daylight.

The high school had been empty, not just for the summer, but since the shooting. The other kids had been moved among the middle and elementary schools, so they wouldn't have to face the trauma of walking those hallways again so soon. It amazed Vivian, really, how far the adults were willing to bend to the shape of that trauma. Acknowledge it enough to reorganize the last quarter of the school year, but not enough to start advocating for change. Not enough to hold the assholes who had let this happen to Cassie responsible.

That was the thought that drove Vivian this time. Her fingers shook with anger. She posted the mural of Ariadne on the account. Ariadne, trapped in her maze, with a monster on her heels. She tagged the same gun control organizations, and the congresswoman who had shared the last post, and the podcast, which she now listened to every new episode of.

Then she sat down and opened her laptop for the first time in months and did what she knew best.

Vivian did her homework.

First, she identified any other members of congress committed to common-sense gun legislation, gathered all their social media handles, and added them to the tags on her mural posts.

Next, Vivian dug into the Violence Against Women Act—which was due to be renewed next year. There was time to close the boyfriend loophole, which made it harder for victims of abuse to get protection if they weren't actually married to their abuser. Made it almost impossible to keep those abusers from getting guns.

Bell didn't want to take responsibility for Cassie.

Bell, *the town.*

Bell, *the family.*

Bell, *the guns.*

So that burden had slipped down, down, until it fell to Beck and Vivian to make it right. To find a new balance, in a world without Cassie.

Vivian had never been one for revenge, but people can be changed. *It would be so easy*, she thought now, to let this consume her. To let it fill the spaces in her life left empty by grief and fear and loss.

There was a soft knock at her bedroom door, and Vivian closed her laptop. She reached up to her map, thinking she'd take it down, but decided to leave it. It was just a map of Bell. Nothing suspicious about that.

It was just her home.

"Come in," Vivian said, and her mother pushed the door open. Vivian's mom, Alexandra, was young. She'd had Vivian just out of high school and raised Viv alone while putting herself through nursing school. It was because of her that Vivian was interested in medicine in the first place. She'd bring home stories from the emergency room—but only the good ones. The time they'd brought a child back from nearly drowning. The time she'd caught a grandpa's heart attack in time to get him into emergency surgery. She'd taught Vivian that medicine was like magic for those whose lives it saved, and Vivian had fallen in love with the idea of it. Vivian, always more grounded in facts than stories, knew that what she wanted most was to be like her mother. Practical, and self-sufficient.

But Vivian also knew that medicine had its limits. Some bodies couldn't be saved from the wreckage they'd faced. Wreckage like a bullet to the temple while sitting in English class.

"I'm heading to work," Vivian's mom said at the door, pulling her back out of that classroom, that day. "There's a casserole in the fridge for dinner. Are you okay, honey?"

106

"I'm great," Vivian said. When she'd first told her mom she didn't want to go to college, her mom hadn't pushed back at all. But Vivian knew it wasn't because she agreed with Vivian's choice. She just figured Vivian needed time to come around.

Part of Vivian hoped that was true.

Another part of her was prepared to risk everything. Her entire future. All those years of planning and studying and *dreaming*. Just to see someone pay for what happened to Cass.

And that part of her was speaking the loudest right now.

"Vivian," her mom said. "The Queens called again."

Vivian turned in her chair. She put her arms around her knees and pulled them in close.

"They really need an answer from you," her mom said. "They want to file this week. Have you thought about it any more?"

The Queens. Cassie's parents. They'd left town a week after the funeral. Not even bothering to sell their house—they just left it standing empty, moving in with Cassie's grandparents on the other side of the state. As far as they could go, as fast as they could get there. But it didn't mean they were finished with Bell.

They were suing the company.

And they'd asked Vivian to join them. For damages. For the health care bills her mother would never repay. For the trauma she'd suffered.

Vivian had been unsure, at first. She didn't care about

the money, and she'd fixated on that—on how others would think that was what she was after. But this wasn't about a payment. It was about accountability.

In this town, owning a gun was the only status symbol that mattered. Town pride. Bell Firearms had designed the weapon that killed Cassie, manufactured it, and then Mr. Bell himself left it in a place accessible to someone dangerous.

"Tell the Queens I'm in. Let's get the bastards."

CASSIE

During the day
I distract myself
by playing memories in my mind.

I remember how Vivian was always moving.
To stay in shape for track, she'd say,
but I think she just didn't know
how to ever be still.

She'd run before school
and at night—sprinting short distances
to keep her muscles warm, *she said.*

We'd meet at Beck's house
and sit on her grandfather's ancient,
paint-peeling wraparound porch,
and cheer for Vivian as she sprinted

up and down the dirt road
again, and again, and again.

We watched her run,
sipping lemonade
made from cheap powder
and sometimes a splash of
Beck's grandfather's vodka.

That drink
and the summer heat
always made us sick
but we drank it anyway.

I tried to yell
motivational things at Vivian:
You're doing great!
You've got this!

But Beck was Beck:
Move it, bitch!
LIFT THOSE LEGS!
Let's see some effort!

Once when Vivian flew past the porch
sweat dripping down her face

looking like Athena mid-battle,
and Beck was two drinks in already
she yelled things like:
Hot stuff, Viv! Bend it like Beckham!
Nice ass!

Then she slipped her two fingers
between her lips
and gave Viv
a nice long whistle.

The next time Viv came
around the corner
she had the hose on,
full blast,
and chased us off the porch with it.

During the day,
all I can do is remember.
But usually the memories
are enough.

MURAL 3

TITLE: **MEDUSA**

LOCATION: **THE WATER TOWER**

BECK

BECK JONES WASN'T ALWAYS SCARED OF heights.

She'd spent so many nights out on the fire escape of her apartment building. She'd drag a blanket out and watch the stars, not bothered by the openness beneath her feet. She just wanted to be out there, in case there was a clear night, cloudless, giving her a view of the stars.

That changed when she was seven.

She'd been outside for an hour, and the window dropped shut. She tried as hard as she could, but tiny Beck couldn't lift the stuck window again. She was trapped on the fire escape. At first she tried banging on the window, but her parents were passed out in another room. They'd been drinking. They were always drinking. So Beck decided to climb down. She took her time, one step at a time on the ladder rung, both hands gripping. But as she walked along the partition to reach the next ladder, the railing broke.

Beck fell.

It was random, the man walking by below. And he could have easily been watching his feet. Minding his business. But the sky was particularly clear that night, and that twenty-three-year-old man had his eyes up, looking at the stars, just like Beck. So he saw her fall.

Somehow, he caught her.

That was how Beck made it on to child protective services' radar. And she never made it back off, until she went to Grandpa's farm. She never sat out on the fire escape again, either. Couldn't even look out of the apartment windows.

And now, a decade later, Beck was climbing for the second time in two weeks. This time, the Bell Water Tower.

"This is a mistake," Beck said, shifting her backpack to look down at Vivian climbing below her.

"We are fine," Vivian called. "Stop looking *down*."

Beck kept climbing, trying to stem the panic she'd felt to see the ground so far, far below. This was higher than the billboard. It was higher than the third-floor walk-up she'd fallen from as a kid, too. How had Vivian convinced her that the water tower was a good idea?

For Cassie, Vivian had said when she picked that location for their list.

And apparently, *for Cassie* had been enough of an argument for Beck.

When they reached the top, Beck scooted back to the

wall of the water container, pressing her back against it. Vivian immediately got to work, pulling out the first paint can, propping up the sketchbook.

"I think this one is my favorite yet," Vivian said.

"It's the easiest design so far," Beck told her. She needed it to be simple, quick. Something she could finish in an hour or less. Beck didn't want to spend one minute longer than necessary on this godforsaken tower. Not to mention, this location was their riskiest by far. They could see all of Bell, and all of Bell could see them. They had to hurry.

"Sit behind me? Please?" Beck asked Vivian, who nodded and moved between Beck and the railing.

Beck pulled her mask into place and began to paint. It was simple, but it would look great up here on the tower.

Tonight's Greek myth was Medusa.

Cassie said that Medusa's story was misunderstood. She was clearly the victim, but was treated like a monster again and again. Blamed for her beauty. Blamed for her own assault. Cursed with snakes as hair and a stare that turns men to stone.

But Cassie said it wasn't a curse, not really. It was a weapon. The snakes disguised her beauty, so no one would come after her again. And the look that could turn men into stone?

"Well," Cassie said. "What girl couldn't use that skill at one point or another?"

Beck outlined Medusa's head. She gave her solid black,

117

unseeing eyes. They looked creepy on the side of the water tower, looking out over Bell. Like she might freeze the whole town in stone.

And then the hair. The snakes.

"Cerulean blue," Vivian read on the side of the paint can before handing it to Beck. "God, remember what a disaster that night was?"

"Like I could forget it," Beck said.

It was last year, and they were celebrating the start of summer with a road trip. They'd even booked a bed-and-breakfast a few towns over.

Cassie had left Vivian and Beck alone to run to the drugstore for something, and they'd fought the entire time she was gone. The room itself was painful to be in. It was like the designer couldn't choose a floral pattern and said *Fuck it. We'll use them all.* And they had. Flowers *everywhere*, but in competing patterns and colors. It gave Beck a headache after ten minutes.

So she was especially grumpy when Vivian started talking about Beck moving out of Bell next year.

"I'm not. Going. To college," Beck ground out while lying on the bedspread stitched with violets and lilies. "I have Grandpa's shop. I'll take it over for him. I'm all set."

"I didn't mean college," Vivian said. "You *love* making art. You used to say you wanted to be a tattoo artist. You could do that anywhere."

"If I can do it anywhere, I can do it in Bell," Beck had replied.

Vivian probably would have argued with her all night. First, because it seemed like she just loved to argue with Beck. And second, because it was weirdly important to Vivian that Beck consider not staying in Bell.

When Cassie came back to the room with bright blue hair dye, Beck had jumped to her feet and grabbed the box. A very welcome distraction for everyone. So they started with the bleach. And then all hell broke loose.

Cassie said it was burning her skin, and she panicked. She was laughing, and running around the bathroom, and shouting. Like she couldn't decide if the situation was more funny or painful. Beck had to drag her to the shower to rinse out the bleach, but they knocked the blue dye off the counter as they went.

It splashed everywhere.

Blue dye covering the peachy-rose bath mat.

Blue dye on the burgundy zinnia wallpaper.

Blue dye staining the purple chrysanthemum soap dish.

They were kicked out of the bed-and-breakfast and had to drive all the way back to Bell that same night. They picked up new dye for poor Cass, whose hair was only half done, a hideous orange-yellow from the failed bleach job. They went to the lake, because it was their spot, and they sat in the beam of Betty's headlights and finished dying Cassie's hair blue.

They jumped into the lake to rinse.

Afterward, they laid their stained clothes on the roof of the van. Beck passed out clothing from the abandoned pieces that never seemed to leave the van—her old soccer sweatshirt for Cassie, shorts and a thermal shirt for Vivian, an old flannel and some leggings for herself.

Cassie had pulled out Beck's art bag, and insisted Beck give them all faux tattoos *to complete their night of rebellion.*

Beck remembered the look Vivian gave her when she finally let her see hers—a bright red fox on Vivian's thigh, surrounded by brambles and thorns.

"He's beautiful," Vivian said, examining her thigh. "Beck, you'd be really good at this. If you decided to do it."

"Thanks," Beck answered, taken aback by the soft sincerity in Vivian's voice. A far cry from her usual bossiness.

Cassie had asked for sunflowers. And that Latin phrase. The one from the last monologue she'd auditioned with after reciting a hundred times to them for practice. *Collige Virgo Rosas.*

"What's it mean?" Vivian asked Cassie that night, taking a sip from the bottle of cinnamon whiskey Beck had passed around while she painted.

"Gather, girl, the roses. It means pick the flowers, while you still can. It's like *Carpe diem.* Seize the day. Or, you know, YOLO."

Vivian coughed, sputtered, began to laugh, more drunk

than Beck had realized until that moment.

"*YOLO.*" Vivian gasped the word between her giggles, and soon they were all helpless. And once they'd finally calmed down, all it took was someone whispering the word again, and they started all over.

They fell asleep laughing, with the headlights on. They had to call Cassie's parents in the morning to jump the van and bring them real clothes. Their stained ones had blown off the van overnight and were probably buried in mud at the bottom of Bell Lake.

"Maybe that night wasn't such a disaster," Vivian said, turning on the narrow platform so that she was facing Beck.

"Maybe it was kind of perfect," Beck said, smiling at the memory.

"Yeah, maybe it was." Vivian shifted closer, handing her the last paint can.

Medusa was nearly done.

Beck had made the snakes blue, for Cassie, in honor of that night. They never did figure out why she dyed her blue hair back so quickly.

But Beck could guess now. There were a lot of signs that something was wrong. It's just that no one was watching for them.

A sudden sound drew their attention, and Vivian looked over the railing.

"Shit, we have to go," she said. "Get your bag. Don't clean up."

It was Cassie, honking the van, and when Beck looked up, she saw it. Flashing lights, and a siren. On the old highway, but heading their way.

They were gonna get caught.

"Shit," Beck said, climbing on to the ladder after Vivian. She grabbed her backpack, but left the paint cans.

It took them two minutes to climb down, the sirens growing louder—closer—with each rung. Beck's heart was in her throat the entire time, sure she would slip.

"We've gotta go," Cassie said as soon as they opened the doors.

And they did. Doors slammed, blocking out the wail of the police car. Beck drove down the service road that led to the water tower and turned back toward town.

"Hurry," Vivian said. "We need some distance. The van will stand out."

"I know, I know," Beck said, going faster.

A minute later, they turned onto Main Street.

They could still hear the siren, but it was distant now. Probably just arriving at the water tower.

Beck wove through the streets, taking the most round-about way to Vivian's house.

"Maybe we should take a break," Vivian said as she climbed out. "That was way too close. If Cassie hadn't managed to honk the horn, we'd have been caught."

"Okay, yeah," Beck said. "We'll make a plan for next week sometime."

"Dammit, I didn't get a picture of the mural," Vivian said.

"Then you better hope the paper covers this one, because there is no way in hell I am climbing that tower again." Rushing down that ladder as fast as she could, with the sirens growing louder and closer, Beck had felt that same hollow weightlessness she'd felt when she fell as a child. Beck was committed to this insane mission of theirs, but she wasn't going near the water tower again.

"I'll figure it out," Vivian said. "Night, Cass. Love you."

She slammed the door, leaving Beck with her ghosts, and her ghost.

"Why'd you change it back?" Beck asked on the ride home, trying to keep her voice light and casual. "The blue hair. It looked really pretty on you."

Cassie was lying on that middle seat again. *Don't need to buckle if you're already dead*, she'd pointed out to Vivian earlier, who had rolled her eyes.

"Not everyone thought so," Cassie said softly. When she shifted on the seat, Beck could make out the faint blue stain from that night. Cassie had slept on the seat and her newly dyed hair had soaked into it, staining it cerulean blue.

It wasn't fair that Cassie's name would forever be known for how she died. Instead of her laughter, her poetry, her voice. Beck wanted to remember Cassie as she was that night last summer. Blue-haired, legs covered in painted flowers, laughing so hard that tears fell down the side of her face.

So that was what Beck imagined as she painted the water tower tonight. Cassie as Medusa—not cursed, but protected by the stony power in her gaze and the wild creatures in her hair. But she wondered if even that could have kept Cassie safe. Beck knew there wasn't any right way to be a girl in this world, but she'd often wondered if there was a right way to survive as one. Once upon a time, Medusa wasn't a gorgon at all. She was pious and pretty. *Vulnerable*, thought Beck. *And they came for her.*

Then Medusa became something different. Something vengeful and terrifying. She wasn't vulnerable anymore. Instead she was something that men and gods tolerated even less. She was powerful. And they came for her still.

CASSIE

We took a road trip,
leaving on the first day of summer
after junior year.
We only went
a few towns over
but it was the farthest
we'd ever gone
on our own.
We were officially *seniors*
so it felt like adulthood.
It felt like freedom.

I remember rolling Betty's
windows down as we drove,
feeling the summer heat,
the hint of a breeze
and wishing it was forever,

our summer, wishing we didn't
have to go back.

Beck dragged us into a shitty pub
and slipped fake IDs into
the back pockets of our jeans.
Got ya presents, *she said.*

The bartender wasn't
stupid, but he also didn't care,
and gave us whatever
was on tap.

We sat outside on their deck
where we could see the river.
We played we were drunker
than we really were,
cuz when you're drunk
you can say things
and pretend it was the alcohol
and not honesty
putting those words
on your tongue.

Like Vivian apologizing
for being mean, uptight,
telling us how

she's scared all of the time,
of wrong answers,
of falling behind,
of getting stuck in Bell
like her mom, who had,
from Vivian's point of view,
given up everything
to raise her.

Like Beck telling us
maybe instead of a boyfriend
she'd get a girlfriend.
Someday.
And laughing into her beer
and spilling it
when I tackled her
in a vicious hug.
I threw my arms around her neck,
which I like to do a lot
because I'm the only person
Beck lets hug her
besides her grandpa.
He's not overly affectionate,
but I am.
I've got hugs to spare
and they all belong to Beck.

They asked about Nico,
and the laughter died on my lips.
I didn't know how to tell them that,
almost eight months in,
it all felt so wrong.

I said nothing about
how we were moving so fast,
faster than I'd expected,
but he told me he loved me
and isn't that what I wanted?
To be loved by Nico Bell?

And when Nico called
right as the sun set on the river,
turning everything golden red,
I texted him that I was busy
with my friends.
But he called again,
and called a third time,
and a fourth, a fifth—
checking in with me
checking up on me.
I put my phone on silent
and when the texts started rolling in,
I turned it off.

That night we dyed my hair
a brilliant shade of blue.
I picked the brightest
color in the drugstore
on purpose,
to remind myself
I was still me.
To pretend that I
was still in control.

VIVIAN

VIVIAN WAS SITTING ON THE BENCH outside of the fire station, staring up at the water tower.

She had a photo of the third mural, the Medusa. She stole it from the *Bell Review* online, glad they'd posted about this one so she didn't have to climb for a photo.

"Cassandra" had just crossed ten thousand shares and twice as many likes, and "Ariadne" wasn't too far behind it. A celebrity had linked to the murals, drawing in a new audience, new comments. There were a lot supporting them. People echoing their call for gun reform.

But the murals, and the attention they were getting, were making a lot of people angry, too.

Vivian needed to post the next one, but she was nervous. It was exactly what she'd set out to do—tell Cassie's story. Get people talking about Bell and its guns. But it was one thing to imagine it and another to see it happening.

Her finger was still hesitating over the button when Matteo stepped out of the fire station.

"Hey, V." He sat down next to her, and Vivian locked her phone before he could see it.

Matteo nodded in the direction of the water tower. "It's beautiful, isn't it?"

"Yeah," Vivian agreed softly.

"I like the snakes for her hair." He kept going, stretching out his long legs, nonchalantly brushing his hand through the mop of brown curls on his head. "You know what's funny?" he asked.

"Hm," Vivian said, her eyes on her shoes and nowhere else.

"That mural on the water tower looks *so* familiar to me," he said, keeping his voice soft and casual. And that was what made Vivian suspicious.

He was *trying* to sound calm.

"Ah, I've got it," he said, snapping his fingers. "That mural reminds me of our school play last year. Remember that? Cassie pulled us *all* in on that one. Made you help with the costumes—those long white Grecian robes, remember? And the backdrop on the stage was that picture of Cleopatra, all dark lines, and her big eyes staring out at the audience. That's what Medusa up there reminds me of."

Vivian looked up then, her eyes narrowing on him.

Beck had painted the backdrop for that play.

"Shit," Vivian said, turning on the bench to face him. "Shit. Matteo. You *know*."

"I suspected," Matteo said, turning to her. "Now I know."

Vivian covered her face with her hands. "Dammit."

131

"Vivian," Matteo said, reaching for her fingers.

He had to peel them down one at a time before she would look at him.

"I'm not going to tell anyone, V."

"I know that," she said. She did. She trusted Matteo. And Matteo had been Cassie's friend, too. "But if you figured it out because of that play, then someone else could."

"Oh," Matteo said. "I didn't figure it out because of the play."

"Then how?" Vivian asked.

"It's your hair," Matteo answered. He reached out, grabbed the end of one of Vivian's long dark braids, and held it up in the beam of the motion-activated spotlight that was fixed on the side wall of the fire station behind them. It flickered on with the movement.

The bottom half of Vivian's braid had blue paint all over it. Cerulean blue. Just like Medusa's braids.

"That could have been from a lot of things," Vivian protested.

"I know. That's why I said I *suspected*," Matteo said with a cheeky grin, and Vivian smacked him.

"Matteo!" she said. "This is serious."

"Yeah, V. It's dead serious. But there's no one else who would risk so much for Cassie's memory. It had to be you two." A moment of quiet passed between them. "They're gonna catch you."

"I can't stop, Matteo. We need to hold them responsible."

"Who?"

"Steven Bell, and everyone who works for him." Vivian knew her mistake the moment the words left her mouth. "Wait, Matteo, I—"

"It's okay, V. I get it." But he rose from the bench and began to pace around.

Matteo's mom worked at Bell.

"I'm sorry," Vivian said. "I didn't mean—"

"You did, Vivian. At least own it. You mean everyone. You're angry at the entire company, the entire town . . ."

Vivian was silent. It was true.

"And so am I."

She looked up at Matteo. "What?"

"How many more do you have planned?" Matteo asked, head nodding toward the water tower.

"Three," she answered.

"You're risking it all for this, Vivian. What about school?"

"I'm not going, Matteo. I'm—I'm not going."

"Christ, Vivian. You're just gonna let them take everything from you?"

"Not *everything*. But right now? Matteo, I can't see past this. This is what I need."

He paced some more, and even though Vivian had known Matteo her whole life, she had no idea what he was thinking of her now. Matteo knelt in front of her at the bench. "Here's the deal, V. I'm going to help."

"Matteo—"

"You're going to get caught. Especially if you keep posting to that account."

"I'm spacing them out," Vivian said.

"That's not enough, and you know it."

"I'm doing the best I can."

"You need help," Matteo said, putting his hand on her arm. "Let me help."

Vivian looked up at him. "No way. We could get arrested. I don't want to drag you into this."

"V. You don't have a choice here," Matteo pointed out. "Besides, I want to do it. For Cassie. I cared about her, too, you know."

Vivian had wondered, before. She noticed the way Matteo had looked at Cass across the lunch table sometimes. In the weeks before Cassie died, Vivian had seen them laughing together at her locker. She figured they were becoming friends, but now she realized it was maybe more than that.

"You don't have to do this all on your own. I know what's at stake, V. It's worth the risk. But if you keep trying, you're going to make a mistake and get caught."

He was right.

And she was exhausted already, and they still had a while to go.

"All right. Okay. You can help," Vivian said.

"Cool. Now give me your phone."

"Why?" Vivian asked.

"V. Give it to me."

Vivian unlocked the phone and handed it to Matteo. He went into her photos, chose a few of the Medusa mural, and texted them to himself.

"You paint. You photograph. You tell me what to say, but I'll do the posts."

"But then won't you just get caught?" she asked.

"I'll do them at the library in Tannersville," Matteo said. "I'll use a public computer. I'll be in and out."

Vivian had to admit, it was a better plan. If they broke up the tasks, and posted them from the library . . . then maybe there was less of a chance of it all being traced back to Vivian and Beck.

She nodded. "Yeah, okay. Thank you, Matteo."

"And I want to help with the next mural."

"No, you don't."

"Yes, I do."

"You won't once you know where it's going," Vivian said with a laugh.

"Try me," he challenged.

Vivian didn't answer. She just waved her hand in the air so the spotlight would flicker on again. It illuminated the bright, blank white wall behind them.

The wall that faced the police station across the street.

"Shit," Matteo said.

WE CAN BE HEROES
SEASON 2: EPISODE 16
"THE PARENTS"

MERIT LOGAN: Cassie Queen was born here in Bell in 2004. She was known for her wide smile, contagious laugh, and her exceptional talent in singing. Cassie had a beautiful voice and was performing in local talent shows and plays from the time she was just four years old. One of Cassie's performances went viral when she was just fifteen, and in January of this year, Cassie was invited to study at Yale's prestigious theater school, in addition to a few other notable acceptances. Today we are joined by Cassie's parents, Patrick and Anna Queen.

MERIT: Thank you so much for talking to me today, Mr. and Mrs. Queen.

PATRICK: Thank you for having us, Ms. Logan.

MERIT: Before we get into a discussion of the lawsuit, I was hoping you could just tell me a bit about Cassie.

ANNA: Of course, yes. Cassie was one of those kids who was always rescuing something. Remember that, Pat?

[Soft laughter]

PATRICK: Of course. She had an aquarium in her room that was always filled with some creature she was determined to save—

ANNA: —she couldn't save them all.

PATRICK: But she tried.

ANNA: Cassie did that with people, too. She had a million friends. She was very loved. I think because she was very loving.

MERIT: She sounds special.

ANNA: She was. But she was also vulnerable.

MERIT: How so?

ANNA: Cassie wasn't naive. But she had a lot of faith in the goodness of people. In the idea of redemption.

MERIT: Do you mean Nico?

PATRICK: Not at first. He was a charming kid. Good student. And of course, we knew his family. We didn't see what it was until Cassie was in too deep, and then . . . then we didn't know how to get her out.

[Extended silence]

MERIT: Can we talk about the lawsuit?

ANNA: We are suing Steven Bell in a civil suit. And we're also suing Bell Firearms, the company, for violating state gun laws.

MERIT: Let's start there. What does that mean?

PATRICK: It means that the company was advertising their rifle irresponsibly. They were framing it as a *weapon of choice.* They advertised its deadliness, and they tied in that advertising with belonging to Bell. Like, you aren't a real resident of that town unless you own one of their firearms. Like you aren't a real man. It was toxic, at best. And at worst . . .

MERIT: Deadly.

ANNA: Exactly.

MERIT: Tell me about the lawsuit against Steven Bell.

ANNA: That one is about negligence. He left his guns in a place accessible to Nico.

MERIT: But the protection order that Cassie got . . . I'm looking at it now . . . didn't request that guns be removed from the residence.

PATRICK: It shouldn't have mattered. Steven Bell had an obligation to keep his guns safe from minor access. He failed in that duty.

MERIT: . . . do you think you'll win? People have tried to sue gun companies before. It doesn't usually go in their favor.

ANNA: We don't . . . we don't know. But we aren't doing this for us.

PATRICK: Or Cassie, honestly.

ANNA: We are doing this for the next family. The next family whose child goes to school and doesn't come home. This isn't about us. It's about accountability.

MERIT: Thank you for talking about this. I know it's difficult. But I was wondering if, before we finish, we could talk about these murals in Bell.

ANNA: Well, we don't know much.

PATRICK: Except—

138

MERIT: Except?

ANNA: It must be someone who loved her. Someone who agrees with us. That all of this isn't about revenge against Bell Firearms. It's about taking responsibility.

MERIT: You think the murals and the lawsuit are seeking the same thing?

PATRICK: I think we all want the same thing.

MERIT: What is that?

ANNA: We want our girls to be safe from anyone who wants to harm them. And we want all our children to come home from school at the end of the day. That doesn't seem like an enormous, impossible request, but . . . but many people disagree with what we are doing.

MERIT: How do you know that?

PATRICK: Well, we've been getting death threats every day since filing the suit.

MERIT: You are going up against a powerful family. A powerful lobby, too.

PATRICK: Cassie had rights, too. And we think that's worth fighting for. Our grief is never going away. But maybe . . . maybe we can keep another family from going through this hell.

BECK

BECK WAS ON THE CREEPER, ROLLING around under Lola Talbot's ancient hatchback, trying to find the source of the weird sound she said it was making.

There was sudden pressure on the end of the board, and Grandpa pulled her out from under the vehicle using his foot. He had a piece of paper in one hand, and the *Bell Review* in the other. It took Beck a moment to recognize the paper as their map of Bell, marked with the locations of all their planned murals.

Well, shit, thought Beck.

Grandpa was silent. Beck could only imagine his thoughts. Maybe he thought that first mural would be the only one. And hoped the same after the second one at the school.

But now they'd done three, and he was holding a map where they had clearly marked three more spots.

"Grandpa, I can—"

"No explanation necessary, Beck," Grandpa said. "It's all

right here in front of me."

He was quiet again, studying the map.

"Grandpa, can I just—"

"The side of the fire station is risky," he said, tugging on the sides of his mustache as he thought about it. "But I'm guessing Vivian would know if you could pull it off, since she works there. But the one after that? Mural number five? That won't do. You'll get caught."

"But . . ." Beck was confused. Grandpa looked up at her over his wide-rimmed black glasses, his mouth pursed and his peppered white mustache scrunched up, waiting for her to speak.

He was helping them.

"But the train station's been abandoned for years," Beck said instead. "It's the most out-of-the-way spot we have on there. We were even thinking it was *too* out of the way."

Grandpa shuffled over to his desk, pulling his oxygen behind him. He laid down the map, and beside that, the newspaper, and sat down on his bench. It had made the front page again—the water tower mural. Medusa and her snakes, gazing with unseeing blackened eyes over Bell.

Beck checked her phone, going to the Cassandra account that Vivian had made and clicking through. There it was, the same image as the paper. Vivian was on top of things.

This post was taking off, too. It was being shared on other platforms. What were hundreds of comments on the last mural were thousands now. And more than fifty thousand likes.

Beck switched over to the Bell Firearms account, and sure enough, it was gaining traction there, too. There were hundreds of comments on their last post, and the conflict in the comments was exactly what Beck expected. There were a lot of people speaking up about gun violence, about Bell and Cassie. But there were just as many pushing back.

Either way, it was a lot of attention, which was great for the message they were trying to send. And dangerous for their own anonymity.

"You're playing with fire now, Beck. People are talking about this. Putting it all together. They're already saying it's a couple of kids. They'll trace it back to you eventually."

"Who is saying that?" Beck asked.

"There's talk in town. At the hardware shop. The grocery store. It was all the buzz at the Loft the other day when I grabbed some coffee."

"You're hanging out at the Loft these days?"

"Hey, I may be dying," Grandpa said. "But I'm not dead. I keep up with the—what did Cassie say? I keep up with the *trends*."

He was right. Cassie did say that.

"It's really important, Grandpa." Beck sat down on the bench beside her grandfather, her hands brushing over the map in front of her. Cassie was still in that van. They couldn't stop.

He sighed. "I figured it was. Which is why I'm thinking the Old Mill instead of the train station. It's also abandoned, out of the way. But it faces those open fields on the Warren Farm . . . you know, the ones—"

"—the ones they use for the Sunflower Festival."

Grandpa smiled, winked. "Precisely."

Beck wrapped her arm around him and squeezed. "Thanks for watching out for us."

"Be careful, Beck. Be really careful here. You are a grown-up now, and these are grown-up choices you are making."

"You don't think it's worth the risk?"

"That's not my call to make. I'm proud of you for fighting for Cassie. That matters, Beck. It matters a lot. But don't give up your whole future fighting the past, okay? You gotta take care of yourself sometimes, too."

"I know," Beck said, kissing his cheek. "I'll be careful."

There was a knock at the barn door.

Grandpa stood, passing the paper and the map to Beck, but whoever it was didn't wait to be let in.

"Good morning, Mr. Jones. Hoped I might have a minute of your time."

It was Steven Bell.

Beck was on the far side of Lola's car, sitting down on the bench. Bell couldn't see her from the doorway. So she slipped down beneath the wide desk, folding the map and slipping it into her back pocket.

What the hell was Steven Bell doing here?

"A minute? I got a minute," Grandpa said, stepping forward.

Mr. Bell reached out his hand and Grandpa walked past it, back to Lola's car, lifting the hood.

"A quick minute," Grandpa clarified without looking up.

Grandpa had never had any love for the Bells.

"I'm here for your granddaughter," he said.

Grandpa stood, wiping grease off his hands onto a towel.

"What do you want, Steve?" Grandpa asked.

"There's an art program in New York. For talented kids. I know a few people on the admissions board, and well, I'd be happy to make a call. See if we can get Tribeca in."

"It's Beck," Grandpa corrected. "And no, thank you."

"You don't even want to talk to her first?" Bell asked.

"If Beck wanted some fancy art program, she'd have applied for it," he said. "She doesn't need your help. And the Jones family doesn't ask for favors."

Steven Bell was handsome and golden-haired, just like Nico. He was fit, and tall, and he usually had a smile on his face. A smile that never reached his eyes.

"It's hardly a favor," Steven Bell said. "It's one phone call. I make phone calls like that all the time. To the art board. To the sheriff . . ."

Steven Bell let the sentence trail off. Let the words linger

144

in the air. The sheriff. The art.

He knew. Or he suspected, at least.

This wasn't an offer for help. It was a threat.

"Anyway, Cassandra always told us how talented—"

"Don't you dare talk about Cassie," Grandpa said, his voice low. "And I said no. Get the hell out of my garage, Steve. I'm busy."

Steven Bell backed away, hands in the air.

"I'm just trying to help. We go way back, you and I."

"Just because I used to work for you doesn't mean you own me, Steve. You've always had a hard time understanding that since you took over the company. That's why I left."

Beck didn't know *that*.

"You are a skilled engineer, Mr. Jones. You shouldn't be running a car shop. You should still be with Bell, designing the next big thing. One of your design ideas is still our top seller."

"And I have to live with that."

"Not for long, I hear," Steven Bell said. "Our company still offers excellent health care. You should come back. Let us take care of you."

"I think that's enough," Grandpa said, directing Bell to the door. "Steve, it's the same problem now that it always was with you. You get what you want, and you don't care who you hurt along the way."

"That's just called being a successful businessman," Steven Bell said.

"It's called being an asshole," Grandpa said, and shut the door in his face.

The barn was quiet for a minute, and then Beck crawled out from under the workbench, still clutching the newspaper in her hands.

"He knows," she said.

"He *guesses*," Grandpa emphasized. "If he knew, it would have been the sheriff here, not him."

Beck was nervous for the first time since they had started this. Not for herself, but for her grandpa. His mechanic shop. His fragile health. And for Vivian, who still had a real shot of getting out of here. Following her dreams, even if she thought she'd set them aside.

Beck didn't want to fuck that up for them.

"What about the other thing he said? About better health care."

"Beck, honey, they could put me up in the presidential suite at Walter Reed—give me better medical care than anyone else in this country is getting—and it wouldn't make a difference to this cancer. Even if it would, a few extra months aren't worth the price of my soul. I washed my hands of Bell two decades ago, and for good reason. Steve Bell doesn't give a damn who gets hurt by his guns."

"Maybe we should stop," she said, even though the words hurt her. Even though she was thinking about Cassie. Maybe they could find a different way to give her that closure she needed.

Unfinished business.

Maybe Beck was right in the first place, and they should've just burned the headquarters down.

Grandpa put his hand on Beck's shoulder.

"He's trying to get *rid* of you, honey. Fancy art program in New York? Bell is looking at unprecedented pressure on his company. And *you* are doing that."

Grandpa smiled, pulled the newspaper from Beck's hands.

"Medusa," he said, studying the photo. "It's good art, Beck. And it's working."

It's working. Beck said the words again in her head. *There's pressure on his company.*

A hundred thousand likes. Debates on gun control breaking out in the comments.

And Cassie's name, repeated again and again, by friends, strangers.

Invoked in the name of change.

Beck took out her map and looked at their next mural, marked by an X and the name of the woman from a Greek myth that Beck planned to paint there.

This one was Cassie's pick.

Andromeda, she'd explained, *was sacrificed to a monster to keep her city safe.*

CASSIE

The story I'm telling them,
the whole story,
from the beginning,
could be the length of an epic Greek poem
called "Things I Kept from Vivian and Beck."

So many secrets. Lies. Half-truths.
It happened quick—I was in
over my head
treading water so hard
I couldn't call for help
even from them.

I watch the hurt in their eyes
as these truths come out now
and it is a dull, throbbing ache
to tell my friends, even now,
even in death.

I didn't tell them
when I started sleeping with him.
I didn't know how to tell them
it happened before I was ready,
before I really understood
what he was doing.

If I'd told them I felt shame
they'd have told me
that the shame belonged to him.
But I didn't tell them
so they couldn't tell me.

I didn't tell them
that the road trip we took last year
was just after the first time
he said he wore a condom,
but didn't,
and I went into that drugstore
for a pregnancy test
and panicked and bought
blue hair dye instead.
I didn't tell them how
I sobbed with relief
a week later when I
got my period.

I didn't tell them
his reaction when we got home.
When he saw the blue hair
and his hand slipped into it.
To move it around, I thought,
because it shone so brilliantly
in the sunlight.

Then that hand wrenched my hair,
twisted against my head,
and he asked how I dared
to ignore him for two days
and come back looking
like this.

I didn't tell them
that I cried when he let me go
and promised to dye it back
or that when I looked across the
hallway, I saw Mr. Bell standing there,
watching us.

I didn't tell them how I waited,
tears running down my face,
for him to yell at Nico
and say how wrong it was
and take me right home.

But all he did was say
that dinner was ready.

I didn't tell Vivian and Beck then.
But I tell them everything now.
I let it fuel their sparking anger,
their determination to
make someone pay.
To make Bell *pay.*
For looking the other way.

VIVIAN

CASSIE HAD ALWAYS LOVED THE TRAGIC heroine.

Juliet.

Antigone.

Eponine.

Gwen Stacy.

So Vivian wasn't surprised when, during the summer they were all twelve years old, Cassie became obsessed with a poem called "The Lady of Shalott."

"So she gets in the boat and dies?" Beck asked when Cassie finished reading it to them. Confusion shaped her whole face, from the curves of her orange-red brows to the wrinkles on her nose, distorting hundreds of soft brown freckles.

"It's romantic," Cassie insisted.

Vivian didn't see it, and for once, Beck agreed with her.

"But why do these women always end up dead?" Beck asked even as she helped Cass drag the rowboat off the back of her grandpa's truck. They waved goodbye as he drove away, and then they began to carry it down to the edge of the lake.

Besides, it didn't matter that Beck didn't understand why Cassie wanted to do this. Because if Cassie—theatrical, emotions-always-brimming-at-the-surface, about-to-burst-into-song Cassie—wanted them to reenact her favorite poem, well, Beck would do it.

Beck did anything Cassie asked.

"They're being punished, for being strong. It's called *symbolism*," Cassie said.

"It's *called* being morbid," Beck countered. Beck's curls kept falling out of her messy bun and into her face, and when she reached up to tuck it back, the end of the boat swung down into Vivian's shin.

"Shit, sorry," Beck said.

"Language," Vivian scolded, glaring at Beck and reaching down to rub her leg.

Beck rolled her eyes.

"Yes, ma'am," she drawled out.

Vivian could have kept sparring, but she let it go. It was summer. The heat was turning humid and sticky, just the way she liked it—perfect lake weather. And there they were, at the lake. Everything was right with the world, as far as Vivian was concerned. Bruised shin and ridiculous friends and all.

In return for Beck's fierce loyalty, Cassie fought hard for Beck. She was the one who insisted that Beck had a soft side. Vivian thought of it more like the underbelly of a cat. They might expose it, might look soft and inviting for a moment, but pet at your own risk. Those claws were sharp and on standby. But Cassie forced the issue. She said it was good for Beck to feel big things. That if the two of them didn't draw her out, she'd be like a clam in a shell buried two feet under mud, churning pearls the world would never see. Cassie saw it as her own personal mission to dig Beck out of the darkness, and was always pulling Vivian into her plans.

Which was how they all wound up at the lake, playing out a scene from a poem, under Cassie's careful stage direction.

Which began with a debate over who should play the Lady of Shalott in the first place.

"It has to be Beck," Cassie insisted. "She has red hair."

"What does that matter?" Beck asked.

"Practically all the tragic heroines are redheads," twelve-year-old Cassie explained with a sigh, rolling her eyes at them like this was common knowledge. "Don't look at me like that. I didn't write them."

"No, you're just obsessed with them," Vivian groaned. The heat was getting to her. There were a bunch of other kids there, on the side of the lake, swinging from a rope and somersaulting into the water.

Vivian wanted to jump in, too.

"If I get into the boat will you leave me alone?" Beck asked.

"Honestly, probably not," Cassie answered with a shrug.

Beck climbed into the rowboat and lay down, red mess of curls sprawled all around her. Cassie nodded, content with the vision of peaceful demise that Beck presented.

But to Vivian, there was nothing peaceful about the image before her. Beck was an angel of vengeance, her hair a ring of fire surrounding her. Beck was something wild and fearsome that she would never fully understand, but that she would always be a bit envious of.

Vivian wished she could let it all go—the pressure she put on herself, the anxiety. The need for perfection. Beck never seemed to feel those things.

Cassie and Vivian set to work, tucking flowers all around her, framing her body with the blooms they'd just pulled from the marshy earth surrounding the lake.

Vivian leaned in close, reaching for the far side of Beck. When Vivian's braid slipped over her shoulder, it tickled Beck's cheek and she laughed, her soft breath on Vivian's neck, and Vivian pulled back, overwhelmed by her nearness. Beck had always kept Vivian at such a distance that she'd grown used to it, and the sudden closeness made Vivian's chest ache with something like longing.

Is this what it was like for Cassie to be close to Beck? To see this softness all the time?

But Beck must have felt it, too, because she jolted beneath her. Sent the flowers flying.

"Nope, can't do it," Beck said, climbing out of the rowboat, knocking their carefully arranged flowers off her as she moved.

Five minutes later, after a brief but ferocious spat between Vivian and Beck, where Vivian called Beck hopeless and Beck called Vivian impossible, it was Cassie as the Lady, lying in the boat, with Beck and Vivian doing a terrible job at pretending to grieve her.

"It should be Beck in here," Cassie said from the boat.

"Shh," Beck said. "You're supposed to be dead, remember?"

"You guys are terrible at acting," Cassie said, opening one eye in accusation.

Vivian reached for the fallen flowers, starting again.

"Ready?" Vivian asked when everything was arranged just so.

With a push, they sent Cassie out into the water.

They stood on the dock and their argument resumed.

They were totally unaware that in the middle of the lake, Cassie's rowboat was taking on water.

Vivian realized only when she heard a splash.

Someone was in the lake, swimming to where Cassie's boat had been just a second ago.

"Cassie!" Vivian yelled, running to the end of the dock.

She'd have jumped in, too, but he'd found her. The boy who swam in after her.

He helped Cassie get back to the dock. Kept his hand on the small of her back while she climbed the ladder.

Nico Bell.

The next day, the paper called him a hero.

It was so strange to Vivian now, to think of how much that one summer afternoon had shaped their lives. That if they hadn't been arguing, Beck or Vivian might have noticed the crack on the side of the rowboat, and not sent Cassie off into the water. That if they'd been looking, they would have seen it take on water, and one of them would have been swimming out to help her. Cassie wouldn't have developed a massive crush on Nico Bell the summer she was twelve.

And then maybe when she was sixteen, she wouldn't have fallen for him so fast. Maybe she wouldn't have fallen for him at all. Nico, the golden son, who grew up thinking that the world was his for the taking. That Cassie was his for the taking.

When the world didn't give her to him, he took her anyway.

Even after he killed her, the headlines were still about him. *Bell heir murders ex-girlfriend and self in tragic modern* Romeo and Juliet.

And it wasn't just the one. So many were like it that Vivian had to leave her phone turned off, because soon any red news alert was enough to make her sick, even when it wasn't about the shooting.

The papers talked about Nico's swim record—one even went so far as to dig up the local article about that day at the lake when they were twelve. They lamented, what could have changed in four short years, to take Nico Bell from a hero to a killer? Vivian knew that answer. Nothing had changed. Nico was the same creature he'd always been—chasing headlines, chasing attention, chasing whatever he wanted and believing he deserved it.

The papers didn't focus on Cass. She was never the hero of their story, tragic or otherwise. She was only the girl he'd killed.

And that was what Vivian had to change.

Cassie's story deserved to be told, and Vivian and Beck were the only ones who could tell it. The only ones who could ask her to tell them the whole story now.

BECK

IT WAS FORTY-FIVE MINUTES FROM BELL to the city.

Beck hadn't been there since the shooting, when Vivian was in the hospital—the same one whose university had just accepted Vivian for their premed program. This time Beck was back for an interview. One she hadn't told a soul—dead or alive—that she was coming for.

She parked Betty on a side street, and grabbed the portfolio she'd brought, full of her art.

The tattoo shop was popular, in a great part of town. They took on one new apprentice every couple of years. And they were hiring.

The interview itself was quick, but they asked to keep some of her pieces. Beck hoped it meant they liked her. She wasn't sure she could accept the job if they offered. The commute would be a lot, even if it was just a few days a week. And she wasn't sure she could leave Grandpa alone, or whether they could afford to hire someone to be there with him when she wasn't.

There was so much she wasn't sure of.

But the murals had reminded Beck how much she loved to make art. Art that lived in the real world, where people could see it and react to it. Maybe even choose to wear it on their bodies.

She'd always loved tattoos. Her mom had several, on her arms, her ribs, her legs. Beck would trace them as a child, following the lines. She'd even had one for Beck. A constellation of stars on her wrist. *Because you're always looking up at them*, her mom had said.

Beck wanted to keep looking up. Looking forward. It was what her friends had always pushed for. *Had* pushed for, until March, when Cassie was gone, and Vivian stopped moving forward. Beck thought maybe if Vivian saw Beck doing it, she'd do it, too. Keep moving. Keep dreaming.

Maybe they could do it together.

On the drive home, Beck couldn't help but remember the last time she'd been to the city. She left as soon as she knew where they'd taken Vivian. As soon as she realized that Cassie wasn't at a hospital.

Not Vivian, too, was the refrain in her head as she drove that day, repeated over and over, nothing but the sound of Betty's tires on the highway as she drove.

Beck stayed next to Vivian that entire first day. She refused to leave for anything, not even food or to use the bathroom. She stayed right beside her.

Later, she pretended to sleep in the chair in the corner, hoping no one would notice when visiting hours ended and Beck remained.

But when the nurse came in to shepherd visitors out, Vivian's mom had hushed her.

"She's family," she said, gesturing at Beck.

The nurse let it slide.

When Grandpa came the next day with fresh clothes, Beck changed quickly in the bathroom and hurried back.

She laid out the other items Grandpa had brought at her request: a hairbrush and hair ties.

Vivian had always been particular with her hair. Her cardigans. Even her notes in class—straight, neat lines of penmanship. Beck had thought it was a waste of time, to focus on all of those details.

But she knew Vivian cared about those things.

When they were kids, it had taken a while for Vivian to warm up to Beck.

Scratch that—she'd never totally warmed up to Beck. Vivian had thought Beck was stealing Cassie away, when they were in third grade and having a *Best Friend Forever* meant *to the exclusion of others.*

But they'd eventually learned to tolerate each other, for Cass. And sometimes, Beck had to admit, she didn't totally hate everything Vivian did.

And the very *first* thing she'd liked about Vivian was her

hair in braids in fourth grade. There was something about the care, the attention, that her mother had put into it, that hit Beck like a wave. Jealousy, she thought, of a mother's touch. But it was more than that. It was how Vivian moved and talked. How sure she was, even then, of what and who she wanted to be. Beck felt aimless in comparison. She had been content with a home. A bed. Safety. Vivian, with her tight, perfect braids and huge dreams, was the person who taught Beck to want *more*.

Beck taught herself how to French braid that same night, watching video tutorials online and twisting her hands around the back of her head at impossible angles. Taking it out and starting over, again and again, until she got it right. And when she wore those braids to school the next day, it was because she wanted Vivian to notice. Back then it was just an ache in her gut that said *look* at me, *hear* me, *speak* to me. She thought she wanted to be *like* Vivian, back when she didn't know what that feeling was. Didn't know how to distinguish one kind of want from another.

She didn't put it together that Vivian had been her first crush until years later, and she'd never tell Vivian that, not now. Because Vivian was *also* her first nemesis, and even now the friendship between them was a fragile thing.

But that was why Beck knew how to braid Vivian's hair just the way she liked it.

So she did, in that hospital that day. When she wasn't

sure if Vivian would survive.

With Vivian looking utterly unlike herself, hooked up to tubes, and a machine breathing for her. *Medically induced coma*, whispered a doctor in the doorway with Vivian's mom. *Lost so much blood . . . don't know the extent of the damage.*

Beck tuned them out. Kept braiding.

When she was done, Vivian looked more like herself. A terrifying version of herself, one that Beck knew she would see for years when she closed her eyes. But she looked like Vivian in those braids.

Beck woke up that second night to alarms blaring when Vivian's monitors started going off. Nurses and doctors rushed in, and Vivian was taken for another emergency surgery on her leg.

The hushed whispers at the door were different after that.

Might have to amputate, said the doctor.

The word was enough to keep Beck up the rest of the night. Not because she was scared for Vivian to lose it. But because if they were debating how best to save her leg, maybe that meant her life wasn't in danger. Beck had one clear wish, one plea on repeat from the moment she stepped into the hospital. *Please don't take her, too.* There were two more surgeries that week to save Vivian's leg, and each one filled Beck with more hope.

There were no surgeries for Cassie.

MURAL 4

TITLE: ANDROMEDA

LOCATION: THE FIRE STATION

VIVIAN

WITH THE LAWSUIT NOW PUBLIC KNOWLEDGE, Vivian couldn't shake the feeling of vulnerability that followed her around Bell.

It was like the stakes of what they were doing were suddenly almost unbearable. Get caught making murals, risk the lawsuit. Stop making murals, and maybe Cassie would be trapped forever. Not that Vivian would mind keeping Cass with them always. But what kind of existence would that be?

There were no easy answers, so there they were, on their way to buy new paint for the next mural.

"Am I just noticing it more, or has Bell really stepped up their advertising since the lawsuit was filed?" Beck asked from the driver's seat.

This drive into Bell was different.

Vivian felt like all eyes were on her when she stepped out of the van. It was the middle of the day, bright and warm, but Vivian felt a chill when a man made eye contact with her, and narrowed his eyes. *It's in your head*, she told herself. *No one knows who you are.*

But the signs were real.

Bell Firearms was advertising, literally, on every corner. They'd distributed signs to businesses in the area—the ones whose owners wanted certain *vandals* to know that if they messed with their property, they would be met with deadly force. Vivian wondered when they had crossed the line into thinking that any piece of property was more valuable than someone's life. The signs were in almost every single shop window, stating "This business is defended by the Second Amendment." With a Bell Firearms company logo printed on the corner.

"Fun fact: Did you know this town has five gun shops but no library?" Beck asked as she parked Betty down the street from the paint supplies store.

"There is nothing fun about that fact," Vivian said, falling into step beside Beck.

Any space that wasn't advertising Bell Firearms was taken up with posters for the Sunflower Festival. It used to be Cassie's favorite thing, but the sight of the posters now just made Vivian angry. They were using it like a Band-Aid on a bullet wound. Trying to pretend that things could carry on as usual, even after what happened to Cass.

Vivian watched her feet as she walked, so she wouldn't have to make eye contact with anyone else. And so she wouldn't have to see those black-and-white signs. Those sunflower posters, promising sunshine and happiness.

But the world wasn't all sunshine.

Vivian knew that better than anyone.

And to see the town responding stronger to the filing of the lawsuit in Cassie's name than they ever did for her death? Well, that just made Vivian more sure than ever that what they were doing was right.

Vivian had been listening to the podcast about gun violence, now focused squarely on Bell. It was all about the history of their town, about what happened to Cassie, and now the lawsuit, too. Vivian had cried through the entire interview with Cassie's parents.

But it was one little snippet of conversation, from the very first episode, that Vivian couldn't get out of her head. It was when the sheriff of Bell had said, "Girls are killed every day," and he'd said it like it was nothing. Like Cassie's loss was ordinary. Expected. Acceptable. The price we are willing to pay, so that everyone can keep their guns.

But Vivian never agreed to those terms. And neither had any of the murdered girls.

Vivian's eyes landed on a sign in a window that was different from the others. It said Don't Own a Bell Gun? Time to Hand in Your Man Card.

And in the picture was a mustache, a beer can, and a gun.

"That's disgusting," Beck said when Vivian pointed it

out. "There are kids walking around here reading that shit."

"Do you think that's what Nico heard in his house every day? 'Be a man. A gun will solve your problems.'"

"Something like that."

They'd arrived at the art supplies store, and Vivian reached for the door.

"No, not the front," Beck said, grabbing Vivian's arm and pulling her around the side of the building.

"What are we doing, Beck?" Vivian asked. Beck was opening the back door to the shop and waved for Vivian to follow her.

In the back of the paint shop was a storage room, filled floor to ceiling with art supplies.

"Wow," Vivian said. "Is this, like, your mothership?"

"Shut up," Beck said, shoving a box into Vivian's hands. "Help me."

"Okay, but do we really want to add theft to our list of crimes right now?"

"We aren't stealing. I know the owner, Ruth. We have an . . . arrangement."

"Shit, Beck, she knows?" Vivian said.

"She's cool," Beck said. "She gets it. I pay her back for everything."

Beck began to add cans of spray paint to the box Vivian was holding, threw in a new box of masks.

"Well, then, I should probably tell you that—" Vivian was

cut off by Beck's hand covering her mouth.

"Shh," Beck whispered. "Someone's in the shop right now."

The girls crept over to the doorway leading into the main room of the store. Vivian could see the owner, an older woman, sitting at the register, a paintbrush tucked between her lips.

Vivian smiled at the sight.

It was like peering into Beck's future.

But it was the men who caught her attention. They were tall, muscular, mustached.

Armed.

One had a long gun strapped against his back.

The other had a handgun visible at his hip.

Vivian felt it like a wave—first nausea, then chills that had her wrapping her arms around herself. She had to step back from the door, and she hit the wall and slid down, making a thudding sound.

"Shit," Beck whispered, pulling back from the door. "Vivian. Be. Quiet."

"Is that all you need today, gentlemen?" Ruth asked. "Just the red paint?"

"That's all," said one of them. "We've got a little art project to do."

The second man laughed on their way out of the shop.

In the back room, where she could no longer see the men or their guns, Vivian's heart had slowed to normal. She'd stopped feeling cold chills all over. She stood up slowly, moving to Beck.

They could guess what the paint was for.

"Beck," she began, but Beck waved her hand, dismissing it.

"It's fine," Beck said. "They were never going to leave them up. Let them destroy them. It just makes them look like even bigger assholes."

Beck left an envelope on one of the shelves, filled with cash to cover the supplies they were taking, and the girls slipped back out to the alley. The box was folded closed, but it still felt strange, to be walking around in broad daylight with all the evidence of what they'd been doing just sitting in their hands.

Back in the van, Beck turned to Vivian.

"You were gonna tell me something. In the back of the shop."

Vivian hesitated.

"Just say it," Beck said.

"I was going to tell you that Matteo knows."

They waited for nightfall to make their way to the fire station. This location was risky. But the large white wall faced the police station across the street, and Vivian couldn't let go of the notion of making the man who'd said "Girls are killed every day" look at a mural of Cassie right outside his office window.

The moment they'd parked, however, Beck was reaching for her baseball bat.

"Beck," Vivian said. "Beck, no."

"I'm just gonna talk to him," Beck said, opening the van door.

"Be gentle," Cass called from the back of the van. "He's a good one."

Vivian ran after Beck and caught up with her in the rec room of the fire station. Matteo was sitting on the couch, and Beck stood in front of him, bat casually resting on her shoulder.

Matteo had his hands up in surrender.

"How'd you figure it out?" Beck asked.

"I'm a very observant person," Matteo said.

Beck tightened her grip on the bat.

"Vivian had paint in her hair. And I know your art, Beck. So do a lot of people. You need to be careful."

"No shit, Sherlock," Beck said, rolling her eyes. "We are being careful. That's why you knowing is a big deal."

Beck lowered the bat.

"Did I pass the test?"

"I haven't decided yet. You are on probation."

"Fine," Matteo said. He got off the couch and circled around Beck, giving her a wide berth.

In Matteo's defense, most people were pretty scared of Beck at first.

Even Vivian had been, once upon a time.

"Come on, check this out," Matteo said, excitement in his voice.

"This isn't a party, Matteo, we're committing a crime," Vivian scolded, but followed him.

"Why can't it be both?" Matteo turned as he said it, raising both eyebrows at them. "Both is good. Besides, rebellion is fun. And you," Matteo looked to Vivian. "You are *long* overdue."

He led them outside the fire station, around to the wall they planned to paint tonight. Beck's drawing this time was of Andromeda, whose father and city had left her chained to a rock, waiting for a monster to devour her.

This mural was one of their less subtle messages.

Outside, Matteo stood next to the wall. He put his hands over his head and waved them around.

"Jesus Christ," Beck said, pinching the bridge of her nose in her fingers.

"Matteo," Vivian said, lifting her arms to catch his. Was he *dancing*?

How had she not known that Matteo was such a bad dancer?

"Matteo!" Vivian had to jump to reach his arms. "Enough. This is serious."

"Course it is," Matteo said. He caught Vivian's hands, and began to wave them around, too. "Vivian, what is not turning on right now?"

Then it hit her.

The motion detector light wasn't turning on.

"How did you . . ."

But Matteo was reaching into his pocket and pulled out a handful of batteries. "I'll put them back later. Also told Joe that I'd clean the truck for him if it was a quiet night, so he left it out."

Vivian and Beck turned to see the fire truck, parked ten feet away and totally blocking a large portion of the wall they were about to paint.

"Okay," Beck said. "You passed the test."

Vivian went back to the van, reaching for the box of paint supplies they'd picked up earlier.

"Told you he's a good one," Cassie said. "Also, turn that song on before you go. I think it's number seven?"

"You *think* it's number seven? You've made us listen to that song a hundred times in the last few weeks. It's number seven."

Vivian tossed her phone into the middle seat of the van.

"And turn it on yourself, Cass. Your ghost powers are stronger than ever."

But when Cassie hit play, it wasn't the music. It was the latest podcast. It had gone up just a few hours ago, and Vivian had been planning to listen while they painted tonight. It comforted Vivian. The podcast. The idea that they weren't alone in this fight for Cassie.

". . . *just learned that Steven Bell released a statement today in response to the murals, calling out their lawlessness,*" said the host, a woman named Merit Logan. *"You know, he's spent more time condemning property damage than gun violence? It's not hard to guess where the priorities are in Bell. That's the way this town has always been. Always. That company first, and then everything else. But today Bell puts out this statement, saying it all again and louder, and this time, he attaches a reward to it."*

Vivian's eyes met Cassie's across the van as the words hit them.

A reward.

"That's right. Steven Bell is offering ten thousand dollars for any information that leads to the arrest of Bell's most ardent artists."

CASSIE

August of last year
before school began,
we stole drinks from
Beck's grandpa's cabinet
and climbed the hill
to the Warrens' farm
for the annual
Bell Sunflower Festival.

They charge admission
but if you can navigate a field
you can slip in for free
and we knew the hills
of those farmlands
better than anyone
after a childhood of summers
spent exploring them.

But when we got to the edge
I spotted his family right away
The Bells.
They looked picture-perfect:
mother, father, golden son.
Mr. Bell was guest of honor
like every other year,
opening the festivities.

I shrank back among the stalks.
Let's get lost in here,
instead,
I said.

They must have been confused.
The festival was my favorite thing
all year.
But somehow they knew,
by the urgency in my voice,
or the way I'd grown quiet
and withdrawn
all summer.

They knew I needed
only *them.*

We drank more, and ran
like we were children again,
ferocious and free.

We were feral things once,
untethered, unburdened
by all the strange,
hard things that come
with growing up a girl
in a world built by men.

That night we ran
like wild things again,
until finally we collapsed,
breathless and drunk,
scratched by the coarse leaves,
smelling like dirt and rum.
We lay on the warm earth
with the sunflowers
like towers over us,
hiding us from all
the rest of the world.

It was her constellation
over our heads that night
in the field.

Andromeda.
Andromeda, whose city—
whose very father—
chained her to a rock by the sea.
Left her as a sacrifice to a monster.

When Vivian passed me the bottle
with a slurred
Penny for your thoughts,
I pointed out the stars above us.

Stop being smart
when we're drunk,
scolded Beck.
It's annoying.

I tell them her story anyway.
Andromeda was left for Cetus,
the sea monster.
She was given to save the city,
but at the last moment, Perseus
swooped in on Pegasus and saved her
and married her.

Let me guess, *said Vivian.*
You are Andromeda,

and Nico is your brave demigod,
coming to save you.

Vivian and Beck were reduced
to laughter and hiccups.
I never finished the story.
I never told them
Perseus wouldn't save Andromeda
until her father agreed
Perseus could marry her.
The same father
who had chained her
and left her to die.

You could argue the king did it
for the good of so many—
to save his kingdom from ruin.
But I'd say he did it to save
his throne. And that bad men
can love things, too.

If he'd sacrificed everyone,
then who would be left to idolize him?
But what was the life of one girl,
reasoned the king.

If the hero dies, they call
it a Greek tragedy,
but when the heroine dies,
it's a romance.

Now I only want stories
where girls are the heroes,
and our fates are neither
written in the stars nor held
in the palm of a man's hand,
but are entirely our own.

Another thing I never told Beck and V
was that if I was Andromeda
and it was our town
that left me out on the rocks
in exchange for its own
well-being, then
Nico was not Perseus,
no matter how he looked the part.

He was the monster.

VIVIAN

VIVIAN LET HERSELF INTO THE GARAGE, where Beck was working late. She drew a deep breath, surprised to realize how much she loved the smell of that old barn. But after a decade running around Bell together—fighting at every turn, but still together—the smell was just another familiar thing. Another *Beck* thing.

"Beck?" she called out.

The garage looked empty.

"Yeah?" came a muffled voice from under the van.

The van was jacked up and the windows were all rolled down. Vivian didn't have to peer inside to know Cassie was there—her blue glow was lighting it up.

Cassie's favorite song was playing from Beck's phone on the counter. Vivian glanced down at the screen and smiled. Beck had left it on repeat for her.

What a softy.

Vivian walked around Betty and dropped to her knees

to look underneath.

Beck was on one of those rolling things they used to get underneath cars. Her teeth on a wrench with her hands buried in the underside of the van above her.

"Give me that before you break a molar," Vivian said, reaching for the wrench and tugging it from between Beck's teeth.

"Thanks," Beck said.

"She okay?" Vivian asked.

"She's got her song," Beck said.

"I meant Betty," Vivian said.

"Betty's great. Just an oil change." As she said it, something came loose, and oil started to pour down out of the van. Beck swore and reached for the little red pail she'd set beside herself, holding it up to catch the liquid.

But it had already splashed all over her.

Beck left the pail to catch the draining fluids and rolled out from under the van. Vivian offered her a towel.

"Hey, thanks," Beck said. She cleaned her hands off, and Vivian grabbed the towel back, wiping the splatter of oil off Beck's cheek that she'd missed.

"You're kind of a disaster," she said.

"What else is new?" Beck asked. Then Beck jerked her head, gesturing toward the far side of the garage. It was dark, and when they stepped into the less used area of the old barn, there was a rustling sound in the rafters overhead.

"Don't worry, it's just pigeons," Beck said. "Probably."

Vivian frowned. "What's with the secrecy?"

"Maybe I'm overthinking it, but pay attention to Cass tonight? She seems, I don't know, kind of blue. *Sad* blue. Not glowing blue."

"Yeah, okay, I'll pay attention."

The girls went back to the van, and Vivian popped her head through the passenger's side window.

"Hey there, Cassie," she called in. She could see just the back of Cassie's head; her long dark curls were opaque tonight, each strand twisting down her back. It made Vivian feel like if she reached out, maybe she could touch them.

She didn't try it.

Beck came to lean on the driver's side window. "Hey, Cass? Maybe we could listen to a new song for a bit?"

"No thanks," Cassie said, without turning around.

"You want to tell us what's bothering you?" Vivian asked.

Cassie finally rolled over and sat up. She looked . . . different.

In one sense, Cassie looked more solidly there. Less translucent than when she first came back to them. Vivian could make out the shape of her jawline, the rosiness of her cheeks. And then she spotted it.

A shadow on Cassie's temple.

Cassie must have noticed, because her hand flew up to the side of her head.

185

"I can feel it there, now," Cassie said. "It doesn't hurt. It's just . . . I'm aware of it."

It was where she'd been shot.

"Can we focus on something else, please?" Cassie asked.

"Actually, I need to ask you guys a favor. Can we lay low for a little?" Beck asked. "With the reward, my grandpa's worried. He asked us to slow down. Take a step back, just for a little while, and I just . . . I really don't want to be causing him any kind of stress right now. Can we take some time off? See if things cool down?"

"Of course," Cassie said.

"Agreed," Vivian said.

"Thanks," Beck said. She finished fixing up Betty and lowered the van down off the jacks. She drove it back out to its new usual parking spot, right next to the sunflower field.

Vivian knew she left it there just for Cass.

But when Beck came back to the garage, just a few minutes later, she looked pale.

"Beck?" Vivian said, jumping off the stool she'd been sitting on.

"V, check your phone."

Vivian opened her phone. She had missed three calls. A dozen text messages, all from her mother.

The messages included a link to the local paper's website.

There was the headline, in big, bold text.

Vivian Hughes: Central Player in Major Lawsuit, but Did

She LIE About Being in the Room Where It Happened?

"What the hell is this," Vivian said, sitting back down.

"It's my fault." Beck croaked out the words, and Vivian looked up.

"What?"

"It says you weren't in school, the morning of the shooting. Because you were in town, buying stuff with your credit card. Only it wasn't you," Beck said. "It was me. I'd left my wallet at home. We got to school, but I was hungry, and Cassie wanted a breakfast sandwich, remember? I offered to go get us breakfast and come to school late. I remember because you rolled your eyes and wished me a happy detention. But when I got to the Loft, I didn't have my *wallet*, and your purse was in my car, so I used your card. And then I used it at the art shop, too. I was just walking around, looking at paint, while Cass was—Vivian, I'm so sorry."

"Beck, why are you apologizing? You didn't print this shit. They're just trying to undermine the lawsuit." Vivian could see the confusion spread across Beck's face.

"You aren't mad at me?" Beck asked. "But I stole your card. I left school. I was going to pay you back, but I forgot about it when I got back to school and saw all of the ambulances and police and—"

"And since then you've been completely distracted, blaming yourself for not being there that day."

Beck didn't answer. Her gaze fell to her feet in shame.

Vivian knew Beck blamed herself for that morning.

She knew it, because Vivian blamed herself, too.

And that was wrong, because neither of them killed Cassie.

"You have to stop," Vivian said. "You being there wouldn't have changed a thing."

"It might have," Beck said. "And you don't understand, Nico—"

"No, it wouldn't. Except maybe he'd have killed you, too. There was no time, Beck. There was no warning. He was just *there*. And then she was gone."

"But Nico—"

"No, Beck. I'm glad you went to get us breakfast that day. I'm glad you were browsing the art store instead of in that classroom with us. Because maybe that's the only reason you are here with me now."

"But you're so angry," Beck said.

"I'm angry at them," Vivian said, holding up her phone, open to the new article. "This is bullshit."

"We can disprove it," Beck said. "With security tapes."

Vivian sighed and patted the bench next to her. Beck sat beside her.

"We can't do that," Vivian said. "We just have to let them tell their lies. It'll all come out in the lawsuit, eventually. But that shop has a security camera out back, too. One that's caught us sneaking in for painting supplies the last few weeks. We can't . . . we can't risk anyone seeing those tapes."

"Shit, you're right," Beck said.

"So we ignore it," Vivian said. "Listen, it's late, and my mom is going to be off shift in a few hours and worried. I should get home."

"I'll drive you."

They walked out together, Beck locking up the garage. But Vivian tugged on Beck's sleeve, making her turn around, pointing to the van where it was still parked over by the fields.

Cassie wasn't in the van.

She was standing next to it, staring at the sunflower field like she was about to walk into it.

Cassie turned to them as they approached the van.

"I learned a new trick," she said with a smile.

"Oh yeah?" Vivian asked. "Is that all?"

"No," Cassie said. "I'm also very cold."

BECK

WHEN IT WAS FULL DARK IN the field, sunflowers lit only by the sliver of a moon hanging in the sky, Cassie got back into the van. She was glowing again, and Beck thought maybe she was brighter tonight. That faint blue tint like a halo all around her. What she didn't know was what it all meant. Cassie getting stronger. Brighter. Leaving the van.

Staring into those fields with that look on her face. That look like longing.

Beck drove Vivian home, and for the first time in a month, the van wasn't filled with the sounds of Cassie's music or the girls' endless chatter. When Cassie had come back, they had picked up right where they'd left off. And it wasn't until tonight that the strangeness of it all had really hit them. Maybe it was the story in the paper. Maybe it was Steven Bell showing up at Grandpa's shop. Or the podcast they'd listened to while they painted, talking about their murals, talking about the movement they'd started.

It was . . . a lot of pressure.

And now there was a reward for their capture.

And here they were, still angry.

And here Cassie was, still dead.

It wasn't fair.

"Look," Vivian said, pointing to the high school as they drove past it. The wall of the auditorium, where they'd painted Ariadne and her maze, was covered in splotches of red paint.

"It doesn't matter," Beck said, refusing to look.

But then they pulled up outside of Vivian's home, and all the air left Beck's lungs when she saw what they had done.

"What the hell," Vivian said.

"Those bastards," Cassie said.

Vivian's front door was spray-painted in big, bold red letters.

LIAR

Vivian just stared, her jaw set, unmoving. Beck could see tears in Vivian's eyes, but not a single one fell down her cheek.

That's right, V, thought Beck. *Don't let them make you cry. Don't give them that.*

"Well, I guess we aren't the only artists in town anymore," Vivian said, her laugh knife-sharp.

"They're just assholes," Beck said. "You were right to file the lawsuit."

"I know I was," Vivian said.

Vivian cleared her throat.

"I'm glad your parents aren't still in town for this, Cass. It's going to get ugly with us going after the company."

"They can handle it," Cassie said. "They're strong. I just wish I could—"

Cassie abruptly stopped speaking, but Beck knew. *I just wish I could see them.*

Her parents and sisters lived hours away now. Beck had thought about driving the van to them one night, to see if they could see Cassie. She'd even asked Cass about it once, but Cassie's rejection of the idea had been swift and severe. *What if they can't see me?* she'd argued. *We'd put them through hell for nothing. And I'll be gone soon. I don't want to break them all over again.*

"I'm exhausted," Vivian said. "I'm gonna go crash. I'll clean the door tomorrow."

She climbed out of the van without another word. On her front step, she moved slowly past the wet, dripping paint. Careful not to step in it and drag that ugliness into the house.

"She's not okay," Cassie said from the back seat, where she was lying down, staring at the roof of the van, staring like she could see through it, right up to the stars.

Then again, Beck didn't really understand Ghost Cassie. Maybe she *could* see through it.

"I know that," Beck said sharply. Tonight had been tense even before the paint on Vivian's door.

Cassie seemed different tonight, too, since they'd found her out by the sunflowers. She felt . . . she felt like she was far away. Aloof. Disconnected.

And that was scaring the hell out of Beck.

Cassie sat up, met Beck's gaze in the rearview mirror.

"So go help her," Cassie said. "Vivian needs you."

But Vivian didn't want *Beck*, and Beck knew that.

"You know, I've been thinking that you aren't such a friendly ghost after all. Cassie the persistent ghost. Cassie the never-stops-playing-the-same-song ghost. Cassie the bossy ghost."

"You know I'm right." Cassie shrugged and lay back down on her seat. "But you can do whatever you want. What do I know? I'm super dead."

Great. Now Cassie was mad at her.

Beck climbed out of the van, annoyed with everything. Especially with herself. It wasn't her fault the paper printed the story. They should have known better. People had to know it was a lie. But apparently not, based on the evidence painted across Vivian's front door.

Beck stopped just outside the open window of the van and dropped her phone on the seat, offering the music app as a truce.

"Thanks." Cassie's voice drifted up from the middle seat.

Cassie had said she didn't want to put her family through losing her again, but what did that mean for Beck and

Vivian? Beck could already feel the distance Cassie was putting between them, and it felt like she was doing it on purpose, giving them space before she was gone for good. They could see her so clearly now, and that shadow on Cassie's head had grown darker. Cassie could move objects with ease. She'd even thrown a sock at Vivian's head the other night.

But Cassie was still there. And Beck was terrified of the moment they'd lose her altogether.

On Vivian's front steps, Beck stopped to find the key Cassie said they kept in a potted plant. Her fingers brushed the paint as she unlocked the door, and came away wet. They must have just missed the bastards doing it.

Inside, Beck went upstairs and knocked softly on Vivian's bedroom door.

There was rustling inside, and the sound of Vivian swearing, and then the door opened, just a crack.

"What?" Vivian asked. "Is Cassie okay?"

"Well, I don't know what's up with her tonight, but she's there. Being ghostly. Haunting the hell out of my van."

Vivian smiled, but it was weak.

"Can I come in?" Beck asked, pressing against the door.

Vivian seemed to genuinely debate the answer for a second.

"Fine," she said, swinging the door open.

Beck gaped at the room.

Vivian's wall, the one she'd filled for years with awards and certificates and running trophies, was stripped, already half bare. And on the floor was a garbage bag, half full.

Vivian was throwing away everything.

"Vivian," Beck began, but Vivian held up her hand.

"I don't want to hear it," she said. "You can help me, or you can go."

Vivian returned to her wall, ruthless. She was tearing down every last bit of her old self. And putting it in the trash.

Beck sank to her knees by the trash bag.

"Vivian, what is this?" She pulled out a letter, addressed to Vivian. "This is from your school."

"It doesn't matter," Vivian said, breathless, standing on her desk chair to try to reach her highest shelf.

"Vivian, this says they're giving you another scholarship. Since you can't run track for them anymore. This is a full academic ride. Jesus, V. Why didn't you tell me?"

"Because, even with the scholarship, we are drowning in my medical bills," Vivian said, more harshly this time. She couldn't reach the shelf. "So. It. Doesn't. Matter."

Vivian fell.

And took half the wall down with her.

The shelf tore off its nails, the plaster under it breaking and crumbling onto the floor, coating everything in dust.

Beck moved to where Vivian had landed, offered her a hand.

"Can you stop now?" Beck asked.

"No," Vivian said. "I can't stop. I need it all out of here, Beck."

"Why?"

"Because it doesn't mean anything anymore. It meant everything to me. And now it doesn't."

Beck didn't say another word, but she started to help Vivian.

She picked up all the trophies. She swept up the piece of wall and the plaster dust.

"You can't hide here forever," Beck said. "Our real lives might have been put on hold when Cassie . . . last spring. But they're not over. You are still gonna be a doctor. You are still going to do all those things you worked so hard for. It doesn't mean *nothing*. The meaning just changed."

"Why can't I hide here? Isn't that what you're doing?"

Beck wanted to correct her. Tell her she was pushing herself, too, pushing past this debilitating grief that she'd been stuck in. Not just since she'd lost Cassie, but longer. Since she'd lost her parents.

But she hadn't gotten that job yet. She didn't know if she had a future outside of Bell.

So she said nothing.

Beck took the bag with her. She was afraid Vivian would walk it right down the street to the dumpster outside the gas station if she left it behind. And she knew Vivian would want these things back eventually. Maybe not for a while.

196

But she'd want them someday.

Beck grabbed a bucket from Vivian's kitchen. Found some gloves in the cupboard. She couldn't find alcohol but grabbed soap and hydrogen peroxide. If Beck knew anything, she knew paint. She'd find a way to get it off that door.

It took her an hour to clean the front door, and when she got back to the van—back to Cassie—that song was playing. The same one. It was always that song now. But Beck didn't say a word about it. She reached down and turned the volume up and sang along.

When Cassie joined in singing, unable to resist, Beck smiled.

Her friends might be hurting, scattered, and aimless. But that was Beck's specialty. They'd spent the last decade holding Beck down, keeping her from flying apart in grief and fear.

She had to do the same for them now.

She had to finish what they'd started.

CASSIE

Betty is parked on the edge
of Beck's grandpa's property,
behind the barn
and right up against
the Warrens' sunflower fields.

Beck let me choose the spot,
and from here I can see the
flowers reaching up,
like children standing
on their tiptoes,
faces tilted to the sun.

But not all the flowers
are blooming.
Instead some shrink on their stems
and the soil beneath

darkens with rot
and when you look closer,
maggots.

Days pass and I watch
the rot spread,
one sunflower to the next.

I don't know if it
was always there
weaving its death through
patches of flowers.
I wasn't ever looking
at the earth beneath them,
I was so fixated on the blooms.

It's hard to notice
changes when they are subtle,
and it's even harder when they
are hidden by something pretty,
so maybe I missed it before.

The same way I missed Nico's
grip squeezing tighter
each time he held my hand,
until it was so hard it hurt.

The way his compliments shifted,
began to contain threats.

Your voice is beautiful
became
You should only sing for me.

I'll love you forever
became
Whether you like it or not.

Be mine *was not*
like the hearts on valentines
that we dropped
into decorated shoeboxes
every February.

And maybe we shouldn't
teach children
that love *and* possess
are synonyms.

The sunflowers remind me
to look closer now.
At the fields.
At the town.

I am realizing now
the danger was always
right there, right in front of me
but I was raised to fear
strangers, not boyfriends.

It was too subtle for us to see
until it was too late.
Too late for me,
and for the sunflowers.
Their stems cracking open
while they're still drinking up sun.

Bell looks different now.

For a while I thought
it was me,
being dead and all of that.
But the longer I stay,
And the closer I look,
The more I see it.

My eyes are on the roots now,
and the roots are rotten.

Because this is a place
that in its own subtle way
decided long ago
the company comes first.

This place is a dog
that's run away from me
and come home again.
I want to greet it,
arms wide open,
this thing I missed.
But its eyes are a little wild
on approach
and when I step too close,
it bares its teeth at me.

It is something possessed,
not loved.
And now it is rabid.
And as good as dead to me.

WE CAN BE HEROES
SEASON 2: EPISODE 17
"THE EDITOR"

MERIT LOGAN: Welcome back, listeners, to We Can Be Heroes. *Let's get right into it. Earlier this week, Congresswoman Maria Roberts went on public radio to talk about guns getting into the wrong hands, and she referenced Cassie Queen and the Bell murals.*

[Audio clip]

"It's great that our youth care. That they're using their voices and their art to send messages about gun violence. That burden shouldn't be on their shoulders. We ought to have addressed these issues long ago. But we can act now. I'm inspired by those murals, and Cassie Queen, and I'll be introducing some new legislation in response to these important conversations around violence."

MERIT LOGAN: Just yesterday the Bell Review, *the local newspaper, published an opinion piece that targeted Vivian Hughes, the eighteen-year-old student who was wounded but survived the school shooting. Joining me today is the editor of the Op-Ed department at the* Bell Review, *Ryan Ripley.*

MERIT: Mr. Ripley, thanks for answering some questions today.

RIPLEY: Happy to do so.

MERIT: Can we talk about this piece you just published, the one about Vivian Hughes?

RIPLEY: The author of the story found evidence that Vivian Hughes wasn't in school the morning of the shooting. That seemed like relevant information to me.

MERIT: Don't you think that another piece of relevant information might be . . . I don't know . . . the medical records that show that Vivian spent that entire week in the ICU being treated for a gunshot wound to her upper leg?

RIPLEY: Of course that's relevant, too. That just wasn't in the op-ed.

MERIT: Mr. Ripley, do you think it was a bit dishonest, to print only the first part of that information?

RIPLEY: I do not. Our readers have every right to verify the news they read in our paper. And we didn't print a lie. Vivian Hughes's card *was* used that morning, at the precise time of the shooting. The writer of the op-ed merely raised a question. One of importance in this lawsuit that could bankrupt a business employing half the town. Besides, health records are protected by privacy laws, so we couldn't have confirmed those details anyway.

MERIT: Do you think Vivian could face retaliation for what was printed in your paper?

RIPLEY: No, I don't. And even if she did, I can't see how the actions of individual readers could in any way be our fault.

MERIT: Even though you printed false information?

RIPLEY: Again, there were no lies in that piece.

MERIT: Only misleading, incomplete truths.

RIPLEY: *Opinions*, Ms. Logan.

MERIT: Opinions *posed* as truths, Mr. Ripley.

RIPLEY: The stakes are very high in this lawsuit, Ms. Logan. We're merely relaying information. Our readers have the right to form their own conclusions about it.

MERIT: Your readers or your advertisers?

[Extended silence]

RIPLEY: I don't understand the question.

MERIT: There is a lot at stake. But I pulled some information on the *Bell Review*. Steven Bell pays for a great deal of ad space, both in the physical paper and online. In fact, Bell Firearms has been the paper's most consistent advertiser for as long as the paper has existed.

RIPLEY: I don't see what that has to do—

MERIT: I'm merely relaying information for my listeners, Mr. Ripley. They have the right to form their own conclusions about it.

MURAL 5

TITLE: CIRCE

LOCATION: THE OLD MILL

CASSIE

Tonight I see Beck
before she sees me.

She's drawn her legs up
under herself
in Betty's driver's seat.
Her wild red curls are
barely contained
in her usual loose knot,
a messy bun
on the top of her head.
Her illegal-midnight-
mural-painting uniform
includes:
an old tee,
overalls,
and a flannel shirt,
despite the heat.

One of her sketchbooks
is open in her lap.
Instead of a drawing,
Beck makes a list called:
"People Who Killed Cassie Queen."

There are many
who would say
that the list had only one
true, rightful name.
The person whose finger
found a trigger
and pulled.

But Beck adds his father,
his mother, the sheriff,
and that deputy, the young one,
who took my statement
that first time at the police station.

Beck writes her own name last.
Underlines it.
Circles it.
Goes over and over the marks
that make her name
until you can't even read it,

scoring the page with her pen until
it tears through, and
the ink bleeds onto the next page.

I don't know why
Beck blames herself
for my death, but
I do know Beck.
And the only person
who can forgive her
is herself.

When she turns the page again
Beck sketches out her
mural for tonight.
Our subject: Circe.

When women in the myths
were born or cursed with gifts—
extraordinary gifts,
ones they could even
use in self-defense—
they became something new.
Not heroes, never the heroes.
They became something to blame.
Medusa had her snakes

to disguise her beauty,
eyes to turn men into stone,
if and when they refused
to respect her boundaries.

Circe had her island,
and her magic.
If I were alone on an island,
I think I might
curse strange men landing
on my shores, too.

I wouldn't have made Nico
a pig, but sometimes I think
he'd have made
a fine mosquito.
I'd want him small,
small enough to crush
on the palm of my hand.

Beck's style for the mural
is the same as the others.
Bold, dark lines.
Simple, clean shapes
form an island with
dark blue waves all around.

Circe stands in the center,
willowy like a tree.
Beck gives her
my ink-dark hair
and ocean-blue eyes.

Circe's arms are full
of the flowers she's gathered,
the island's treasures,
to hide from the men
who came to steal them,
the men she transformed
for their trickery.
Beck fills in the island,
pink,
adds sharp black lines
to form a sea of snouts
and ears,
and round bellies.
Pigs all around,
surrounding Circe,
trapping her in
her very own home.

On the side of the mural,
Beck adds words rising out

of the sea.
Collige Virgo Rosas.

Gather, girl, the roses,
while you still can.

Gather them all,
before angry gods,
and sullen kings,
and jealous men,
and ravenous monsters
(but I repeat myself)
come to take
them from you.

BECK

"YOU'RE NOT AS SNEAKY AS YOU think you are," Beck said to the ghost in the back seat of her van.

Cassie appeared in the rearview mirror.

"Can you do that when you want to now?" Beck asked, and Cassie smiled at her, proud.

"I guess haunting takes practice."

"Well, you've got the time," Beck said, and she didn't like the way Cassie's eyes dropped at the words. "Don't you?"

Cassie didn't answer, and then Betty's passenger door was wrenched open.

"Almost ready?" Vivian asked.

Tonight's mural was going on the old mill, at Grandpa's suggestion. Of course, that was before the reward. The added attention and the added risk. Before Grandpa asked them to stop for a while, and let things cool off, and Beck had only given it a few days. She wanted to wait longer, but the reward wasn't going away, and the op-ed and the paint on Vivian's door had made her more determined than ever.

There had always been risk in this plan of theirs. That wasn't enough for her to stop. And this wasn't just for Cassie, but for Vivian, too. Grandpa didn't know about the red paint streaked across Vivian's door. The trophies and awards tossed into a garbage bag. The scholarship that would go to someone else, all because Vivian couldn't escape the nightmare that Nico Bell had thrown her into.

Beck had to fight for her friends. She had to.

None of that reasoning made Beck feel less guilty for going behind her grandfather's back to keep painting. Beck turned, looking up at the farmhouse. At dinner tonight, he'd thanked her. For taking a step back from everything. "I know it's not easy for you to sit on the sidelines, even for a few weeks."

She had waited till Grandpa fell asleep and snuck out again. She hated to leave him. Hated to lie to him.

But there was still a ghost haunting her van. Cassie deserved them seeing this through. And with the way Cassie had been acting—her strange, eerie aloofness—Beck was afraid she'd slip away from them, not moving on, but just trapped forever in this strange limbo of hers.

Beck felt the ominous ticking of a clock, and she couldn't ignore it. She started the van before she could dwell on the pit in her stomach, the one that told her that whatever her reasons or justifications were, she was going against her grandfather in this.

The drive was short—the old mill was just two properties away, diagonal from the Warrens' largest sunflower fields, and across from the open space on their farm that they let the town use for the annual Sunflower Festival. It was just days away now, and everything was already set up. It was sprawled out much the same as any county fair—the center point was an ancient Ferris wheel that Beck thought looked like a death trap. There were game booths, and the sunflower maze, which had been cut into the field by Mr. Warren.

Just like every other year.

Beck considered talking to Vivian about her worries. About Cassie. Her fear of losing her again, too soon. Or about the distance she was creating between them. But it hurt too much, so she said nothing. They quietly lined up the paint cans. Vivian propped up the sketchbook for Beck. But if Beck had inherited anything from her parents, it was avoiding things that should be talked about, and she didn't even know where to start.

The moon was only a crescent sliver in the sky, which made painting harder, but also lowered the likelihood of someone noticing them if they drove by.

"We should work fast tonight," Vivian said, her mind clearly also on the concept of getting caught. There were patrols out. Not just police, but men in trucks. They'd been interviewed on Channel 6, the local news station. They said they'd find the vandals, catch them, get that reward from Bell.

There was more danger tonight.

"It's simple enough." Beck began with the island, a large, misshapen black circle. She sprayed blue waves around the island, and made quick work of Circe, tall and graceful, standing watch over the island. She made her look like Cass. And then she surrounded her with the pigs. All of the pigs, so tightly packed that they blended together into a sea of them. She painted the island pink, then added in curves for bellies, triangles for ears, and round little snouts. An hour before, it was just blank, whitewashed, dirty stone. Now it meant something. Beck liked that feeling.

"This one feels different, doesn't it?" Vivian asked, stepping back from the wall. "It feels like an accusation."

"Circe. And don't they all?" Beck asked.

"This isn't *one* monster. *One* vengeful god. *One* bad man. This is a swarm of them. Men who aren't entirely evil. They just agreed to go along with the evil things that others did."

"They're still guilty as fuck," Beck said.

"I didn't say they weren't," Vivian whispered. Then she craned her neck back farther. "Look at all of them."

Beck looked up.

It was a perfect starry night. It was like the whole universe was out, hanging just over their heads. It made Beck feel small, but powerful. Like being the last little piece in a thousand-part puzzle. Such a tiny thing, but the rest isn't complete without it.

The stars always made her feel like that. Like she was home.

"Do you still want spaceships to come for you?" Vivian asked softly. In any other time, that question would be mocking. It would have an edge to it—a challenge buried in the words. But the longer they spent together now, without Cassie, the fewer barbs made it into their conversations.

"You know what's even scarier than aliens existing?" Beck asked, still looking up.

"What?" Vivian asked, and then there was the softest gasp, an intake of breath, when a pair of shooting stars crossed overhead.

"Aliens not existing," Beck said, and Vivian rolled her eyes.

"No, hear me out," Beck continued. "Imagine it. Look up at that, and imagine that in all of that vastness, there is no one else. There are a quadrillion stars out there. That is one followed by twenty-four zeros. A number we can barely fathom. Imagine in all of that great, vast, endless space, we are *alone.*"

Vivian looked over at Beck then. "You're right. That is scarier."

They began to clean up the paint. Beck ran back to turn on Betty's headlights, to illuminate the mural for a good photo before they got the hell out of there.

She turned the keys.

It rumbled. Didn't catch.

Beck tried again.

It turned over and over.

Betty's battery was dead.

"Shit," Beck said. "Cassie, the van's dead."

But Cassie was in the far back of the van, looking out at the road.

"Cassie?" Beck asked.

"It's too late anyway," Cassie said.

"Why?" Beck turned in the seat, saw what Cassie saw.

Someone was coming.

The passenger door opened and Vivian threw the back-pack of empty paint cans in. "What the hell, Beck? There's a car on the road. We've got to *go*."

"Betty's dead," Beck said. She tried one last time, turning the key. It turned and turned and didn't catch.

"So fix it!" Vivian said. "You are an actual, literal mechanic."

"She needs a jump," Beck explained. "It's the battery. We left the radio on for Cass."

"Shit." Vivian turned in her seat. It was too late. The car had turned toward the mill. It would be there in seconds. "You know the point of having a getaway van is that it has to be able to *get away*, right?"

The car pulled up beside them. Not a cop. And then a woman climbed out of the driver's seat.

Vivian's door was still open, and they sat there in anxious silence. They were caught. All that work, and they got caught because of a drained battery.

"Hey," the woman said. She smiled at them. "You girls need a jump?"

An hour later, Beck and Vivian sat in the Loft.

Betty was parked down the street, this time with a phone playing music for Cass instead of the radio.

And across from them was Merit Logan.

It had been a tense few moments when they met, with Beck and Vivian thinking it was someone after the reward, someone there to turn them in. But Merit had jumped the van, offered them her card, and asked if they could go somewhere and talk.

Beck and Vivian fought the entire drive over.

"She's talking about Bell, and gun violence, and the murals," Vivian said. "She can help us. She's on our side."

"You don't *know* that," Beck countered. She wasn't used to being the cautious one out of the two of them. But from the start of this, Vivian had just kept leaning further and further into their plans—the murals, taking down Bell—with no thought to the potential ramifications. "You need to be careful, V. Not just for your sake. If you get caught it could fuck up the lawsuit."

"Fine. We'll let Cassie decide," Vivian said, sinking back

into the passenger seat and crossing her arms.

"Casper?" Beck asked softly.

Cassie leaned forward, her soft glow illuminating both of them in the front seats. "I think we need to find out what she has to say to us," Cassie said, and Beck swore under her breath.

It was one more risk. And they were already risking so much.

"She's been talking about the murals," Cassie said. "Giving our little platform big boosts. She's the reason the paintings have national attention. The reason Bell is so scared he's set a reward. I think . . . I think we can trust her. I *want* to trust her."

"Fine," Beck said, knowing she was outnumbered.

She would go.

That didn't mean she trusted her.

When Merit sat down, she placed a notepad on the table, but left it closed, with her pen resting on top.

Merit Logan was younger than Beck had realized. Not long out of college. Early- to midtwenties. She had straight black hair, cut to just above her shoulders, and it swung back and forth when she moved her head. She had bright brown eyes, eyes that sparked with something. *Excitement*, Beck thought. *But why?*

"I've been looking for you," Merit said, lifting her hand to run her fingers through her hair. Maybe it was nervousness, not excitement. Either way, Beck's guard went up at her words, and it must have shown on her face.

"Not like that," Merit said. "I'm not going to tell a soul who you are. I really just need some information. For my show."

"Why?" Vivian asked.

"Would you accept that this series I'm covering isn't exactly what it appears to be?" Merit asked.

"Well, it's been pretty clear from the start that you are in *favor* of gun control," Beck said. "But that wouldn't surprise anyone."

"Look, I know it's clear that I have an agenda here," Merit said. "But it's not what everyone thinks it is. The gun lobby is massive—bigger than one man, or one company, or even one entire town. If I was going after gun control, I'd be in way over my head. My target is . . . smaller. More focused. And it's personal. But now I need your help. I need more information."

"About what?" Beck asked.

"About Cassandra," Merit said.

Beck scooted her chair back from the table. "I knew it. She just wants the same sordid details that others wanted. Details about Nico."

"Wait." Vivian and Merit spoke at the same time when Beck rose to leave.

"Stay," Merit said. "Please."

"I want to hear her out," Vivian said.

Beck sat back down, and Merit looked around. But it

was late for Bell on a Wednesday night. There was no one else there.

"All I have are the official police reports," Merit said. "Of course, they don't mention Mr. Bell, but I need to know—was he involved in any way with how the police responded to Cassie? Was he there? Did they mention him? I need to know what happened when Cassie went to the police."

"Which time?" Beck asked.

She saw the question take Merit by surprise. No one knew that detail. No one knew that when Cassie filed for a protection order in March—two days before Nico killed her—it was her second time going to the police.

"Those bastards," Merit said, her dark eyes narrowing. "Okay. The first time, then. Please."

"Why should we trust you with Cassie's secrets?" Vivian asked.

"Would you trust me with Cassie's secrets if I told you mine?" Merit asked.

Vivian and Beck looked to each other, and Beck nodded her agreement.

"Because I'm going after Steven Bell," Merit confided. "And I need your help to get to him."

It was a bad New Year's Eve by any measure.

But Beck getting wasted before nine p.m. wasn't a great start.

224

She'd spent the entire day in the hospital with Grandpa, waiting mostly, while they ran tests. Tests that gave them a prognosis that had sent Beck right over the edge of her self-control. Her self-containment. The doctors had called it *nothing else we can do.*

Months, they said. *At best.*

They told her to go home and rest, and pick him up the next afternoon.

When she left the hospital, Beck felt like she was coming apart at the seams. She needed Cassie. Maybe even Vivian, too. So instead of going home, she drove right to the New Year's Eve party that Nico had invited them to. When she couldn't find her friends, she started drinking. When drinking didn't help, she drank more. It's not like she knew a better way, not then, not before she'd finally gotten a therapist to work through it. Before that it just felt like self-destruction ran in her family. And that was how Vivian found her: stumbling through the Bells' kitchen, a half-full bottle of vodka in one hand, red Solo cup of beer in the other. Beck didn't remember the details, really, but she remembered Vivian's eyes flashing with something dangerous, angry.

Vivian dragged Beck into the bathroom, slamming the door behind her.

"Where's Cass?" Beck drawled out, leaning over the bathroom sink. The room was spinning, and she closed her eyes tight against the wave of dizziness she felt.

"With Nico."

"Of course," Beck said. Cassie had Nico. And singing. Vivian had college. Vivian would go and do everything she said she was gonna do, Beck knew it.

And Beck would still be here.

Worse, she'd be here alone.

"You *drove* here, Beck. How were you planning to get home?" she demanded.

"With you?" Beck asked.

"Good thing I came tonight. I was going to stay home and—"

"Study," they said together.

Vivian's glare was terrifying, even by Vivian standards.

"You could learn something from how hard I study. God knows how your grandpa's shop is going to survive when you take over."

Of course, Vivian didn't know. She didn't know he'd been sick. Didn't know the diagnosis. She definitely didn't know that Beck had spent the entire day hoping for a miracle and been delivered the worst-case scenario for her grandpa's cancer.

So Vivian couldn't have known that those words would ruin her.

She collapsed into tears, sinking down onto the bathroom floor.

"Beck?" Vivian asked. Beck had never cried in front of her before.

She had never cried in front of anyone.

Beck blamed the vodka.

In a moment, Vivian was right there with her, her hands on the back of Beck's head, her fingers tangling in the mess of Beck's curls. "Beck? Oh my God, Beck, I'm sorry."

"He's dying, Vivian. He's sick, and he's dying, and there's nothing else we can do. He won't be here next year. And neither will you. Or Cassie. And I can't—" Beck broke off, buried her face in her hands.

Vivian stayed there, crouching on the floor next to Beck. She didn't rush her or tell her to stop crying.

"I'm so sorry," she said. And she just stayed there, crouching uncomfortably on the floor, never letting go of Beck while she cried.

When Beck finally calmed down, Vivian had to carefully extract her fingers so she wouldn't pull Beck's hair. She dumped Beck's beer down the drain, rinsed the cup, and filled it with cold water. She sat next to her, and made Beck drink the whole cup and then another one. She ran her hand over her back in soothing circles.

"Why are you being nice to me?" Beck asked.

"Because you annoy the hell out of me. But I love you."

That's when Cassie came flying through the door.

Beck and Vivian sprang apart like opposing magnets, and Vivian was on her feet a half-second later. "Cass?"

"I said don't *touch* me. We are done!" Cassie screamed,

slamming the door and locking it.

"What the fuck?" Beck had yelled, climbing to her feet. "Cassie?"

Cassie stepped back from the door, her arms shaking where they were wrapped around her body.

Her oversized sweater slipped down her arms.

Beck gasped, reached for Cassie. There were bruises all over Cassie's upper arms. A bunch of them, forming a half circle, one on each arm, almost like . . .

"Are those fingerprints?" Vivian said, stepping forward and tracing the blue-and-purple marks, her touch gentle. Cassie still shrank away from it.

"What the *fuck*, Cassie," Beck repeated, and this time the words were a statement, not a question. Beck's hand went to Cassie, too, her fingers lining up along one of the bruises. She realized that whoever had done this had hands much, much larger than hers.

A fist began pounding on the door.

"Cassie!" Nico said through the door, and through what sounded like clenched teeth.

"Cassandra. Do not. Run away. From me." Each phrase was punctuated by a fist slamming on the door, and Cassie moved back a bit more with each thud.

"Shit," Vivian said, snapping into action. "We need to get out of here. Now. Step back."

Vivian swung the door open and went toe-to-toe with Nico Bell.

He looked taller than ever to Beck that night. Six three and built lean and strong from all his years of swimming.

He was huge compared to Cassie. Why hadn't she ever noticed that before?

"Get out of my way, Nico," she said. Her voice was strong, unwavering, and Beck knew that if she wasn't so drunk it would be her standing where Vivian was, standing up for Cassie. But Beck was too much of a disaster in her own right to do anything but pull Cassie along, tugging her sweater up to cover her bare arms, steering her toward the door.

Nico must have thought Cassie was alone in the bathroom, because he stepped back in shock, giving Vivian the wide berth she demanded of him.

"Go away, Nico," Vivian said, taking another step forward, forcing him to either touch her or step back.

Nico stepped back.

Beck didn't wait. She grabbed Cassie, beelining her through the party to the van outside.

Vivian caught up to them a moment later, holding out her hand.

"Keys," she said, and Beck gave them over.

Beck climbed into the back seat with Cassie.

For as long as they'd been friends, it had always been Cassie taking care of Beck. Helping her settle into Bell. Giving her those Cassie hugs. But Beck wrapped her arms tight around Cassie that night.

Cass didn't cry the whole drive, she just seemed cold, and

distant, and for some reason Beck thought that was worse.

Vivian drove to the lake.

She shut off Betty's engine and leaned her head on the steering wheel for a moment. Then she turned to the back seat.

"Okay, so. Tonight was a shit show. And we are going to take this one step at a time."

Beck and Cassie nodded together.

"Cassie. Please talk to us. Please tell us what the hell that was back there."

Cassie sat up a little taller, and when Beck looked at her, she could see Cassie coming back to them.

"That," Cassie said, "was Nico."

"The bruises?" Vivian pressed on.

"I was talking to Ethan the other day. We were just . . . we were just laughing together. I tripped over his foot onstage during rehearsal, and it . . ." Cassie trailed off, looking out at the lake. It was so quiet in winter. Frozen on the edges. Still.

"Cass?" Beck asked, pulling her back to them again.

"He came down the hall while we were laughing, and he didn't say a word. Just grabbed my arms. Grabbed them so tight. He pulled me into the closet and was screaming at me. Accused me of flirting with guys. Cheating on him. It was . . . it went on for a while, and he wouldn't let go." Cassie's arms had crept up, holding the same places where Beck knew those bruises were.

"I thought he would apologize tonight. He's always

apologized before when he—when we fight. But when I told him that he'd hurt me, he started flipping out. Right in the living room, with everyone dancing and drinking. He started to yell at me again, said he wouldn't have to be like that if I didn't act like such a slut with every guy."

"Jesus, Cassie." Vivian sighed. "How long has this been going on?"

"Oh . . ." Cassie looked like she was thinking back, thinking back to the first time. Beck thought she'd say that was the first time. Or a few weeks ago. That something had happened suddenly, that Nico had changed into this . . . this monster. But that's not what Cassie said.

"Always? He's always been like this," Cassie answered. "He's gotten more physical. But the jealousy, the possessiveness, that was there . . . right at the start. And tonight, I just ran. I didn't even know you guys were in the bathroom, I just wanted to get away from him, his ugly words. I'm so—" She hiccupped, stopped short. "I'm mortified."

"Why are *you* mortified, Cassie? Nico is the fuck-up," Beck said.

"Should have broken it off months ago," she said. "Kept making excuses. Forgiving him."

"We should have seen it, Cass. We should have helped you." Vivian climbed into the back seat and sat on the other side of Cassie, sandwiching her in, putting her arm around her. "But we've got you now. And that fucker isn't coming anywhere near you."

"You don't understand, he's Nico Bell. He doesn't get in trouble. And I can't say anything, or I'll ruin his—"

"*His* future?" Beck interrupted. "Cassie, he scared you. He *hurt* you. Those were his actions, his choices. Fuck him."

"Cassie, I think you need to go to the police," Vivian said gently.

"There has to be another way," Cass said, with a hint of something like panic in her voice.

"Of course there's another way," Beck told her. "We cut his fucking hands off for touching you."

Cassie looked to Vivian then for help. But coolheaded, practical Vivian was nodding right along with Beck. "Which of those two options do you think will fuck up his swimming career more?" Vivian asked.

Cassie laughed, a harsh, angry sound. Nothing like her usual one. But it was something.

"God, you're right. I know you're right. Okay. Let's go."

As Vivian drove, Cassie seemed to gain more confidence. Beck thought it was the way they were a united front—her and Vivian—never wavering for a second that going to the police was the right thing to do.

Vivian took Cass in, leaving Beck in the van because she was still drunk.

When they came back out, Cassie had a few slips of thin paper in her hands. It seemed like such a paltry little thing, to keep her safe from a boy like Nico. From a family like the Bells.

"Did you file a report?" Beck asked.

"No," Cassie said. "It wasn't necessary."

"What the hell does that mean?" Beck pressed. "What happened?" She directed that question at Vivian.

"They didn't let me go back with her," Vivian said.

"They listened to me," Cassie said. "The officer said he'd go talk to Nico first thing tomorrow. And he gave me some pamphlets, for counseling, and resources and stuff."

Beck wanted to protest more, but the van was freezing cold, and she was still drunk, so she let Vivian drive them home, insisting that they would all talk about it more in the morning.

They crashed at Beck's house, climbing all together into her huge bed. Beck lay in the dark, looking up at the stars painted across her ceiling. They held Cassie till she was asleep, and then Beck felt Vivian's hand slip into hers and squeeze. She didn't have to say anything, but Beck knew she was remembering how the night started. Beck's grief over her grandpa. She hadn't forgotten, that squeeze said. But for now, Cassie needed them most.

But even then, they were scared of all the wrong things. Or maybe they just weren't scared enough. Because the worst of Nico Bell was still coming right for them.

CASSIE

There was something
about stepping into
the police station
that made me feel guilty.

It was gray and then more gray,
and I can't explain
the urge I had to run
at the sight of the first officer.

Me, who had never so much
as taken a turn without
the signal
or slipped a lipstick
into my pocket
at the drugstore.

Cassie Queen was
a good girl.
But what good
was that for
in the end?

The chair they put me in
was too big
and that made me feel
so, so small.

They didn't let Vivian
come back with me
and that made me feel
so, so alone.

He brought me water,
but it wasn't as cold
as the chair I was in
or the table
my elbows rested on
and I shivered as I waited,
thinking maybe it was the chair.
Does sitting in the same
seat as a criminal
make you feel like one?

He took my statement
without interrupting
and said kind things
like take your time.
When I said that Nico
told me he'd kill me
if I tried to break it off,
he said, I'm sorry that this
happened to you.

It wasn't until he asked
for the name of the boy
who did this to me that
his body language changed.

His eyes still looked concerned
but the concern was
no longer for me,
so he couldn't meet my gaze.
He looked anywhere else.

He was worried for himself,
his job.
Because now I wasn't
just any girl coming for help—
I was complicated, at best,
and at worst, a threat.

I was there asking them
to arrest the son
of their idol.
The man who pulled
all the strings
in town.

The next thing he said was
Could you excuse me
just for a moment?

It might have been an accident,
him leaving the door ajar.

Or it might have
been on purpose.

I could hear him
tell the sheriff who I was,
that I was there
to file against Bell.

Steven?
the sheriff asked first,
and the officer
said, No,
the son.

I remember how the sheriff
didn't sound surprised
when he thought it was
Mr. Bell.

Just a report?
asked the sheriff.
Thompson. Or Thomas.
I remember his signs
on the Bells' front lawn
when he ran for reelection.

It won't be too complicated,
as long as she doesn't
request a protection order,
the sheriff said.

We'll see what she decides,
said the officer,
the kind one,
after she meets with
the advocates
from the clinic.
The clinic?
Why would we call them?

We always do,
for domestic violence,
said the officer.

This isn't domestic violence,
the sheriff said.
And laughed.
I remember his laugh.
It's puppy love. Theatrics.
No need to call them in
and blow this out of proportion.
And if she doesn't file,
no need for a report.
I don't want a paper trail
back to Bell.

The press would have
a field day.

Yes, sir,
said the officer,
the kind one,
who minutes ago
told me he was so sorry
for what I'd gone through
with Nico

(before he knew Nico's name).
Who had encouraged me
to call him by his first name,
like that made us friends,
like that meant
he would help me.

But in that moment,
with the sheriff's cold laugh,
I actually felt relieved.

I thought, maybe,
if they aren't worried,
it's not so bad.
Maybe he's not dangerous.

So when the officer came back,
I told him I wouldn't be
pressing charges
against Nico.
And then he looked relieved, too.

I told him I just wanted
Nico to leave me alone,
and he promised me that
he would personally go
talk to him.

Tell him to give me space.

I thought it was my path
out of the mess Nico
had made of my life.
A way forward
without ruining his.

Without theatrics.

Without the feeling of stares
aimed at my back
for going after
the beloved Bells'
beloved son.

But now I see it differently.

I see that while
they were protecting Nico
and while I was protecting Nico,

No one was protecting me.

VIVIAN

AFTER THE INCIDENT ON NEW YEAR'S Eve, it took Nico less than eight hours to come after Cassie again. Vivian woke to shouting, bleary-eyed and exhausted from the late night before, spent in the waiting room of the police station. Vivian rolled out of bed, checked her phone. It was early. She pulled aside the curtain of Beck's window.

Nico.

"Cassie!" he was yelling. *"Cassandra!"*

His movements were volatile. Vicious. He circled around to his car, kicking at the wheels.

Beck's grandpa was still in the hospital—he'd spent the night. So it was just the three of them at the house. Nico was wearing the same clothes as the night before. If Vivian wasn't mistaken, he still looked half-drunk.

Cassie awoke, came to the window beside Vivian.

"Cassie!" Nico grew softer when he saw her. "Come down here. We need to talk. Cassie, please. There's been . . . there's been a huge misunderstanding."

Beck had woken up, and was pulling Cassie back from the window, turning her in her arms, making Cassie look right at her.

"Do not come downstairs. Do not come outside. I'm going to get rid of him." And then Beck pushed Cassie into Vivian's arms. "Keep her *here*."

Vivian and Cassie sat in the deep-set windowsill. They watched together as Beck stepped out into the yard with Nico. She was holding a baseball bat.

Cassie leaned forward, easing the window open to hear what Beck was saying.

". . . last time, Nico. Don't come back here. Don't go to Cassie's house. Don't look at her in school. Leave her. The fuck. Alone."

"Seriously, Beck? A baseball bat? You think that's going to stand up to what I have?"

Nico lifted his shirt, showing Beck the gun he'd slipped into the waistband of his jeans.

Cassie sucked air in sharply beside Vivian, and Vivian squeezed her hand extra tight in response.

They were silent, eyes trained on Nico.

He dropped his shirt back down. "You know *exactly* who I am. Don't fuck with me, Beck. I can ruin everything you love." He looked pointedly at Beck's grandpa's barn then. His shop. Their livelihood.

"The only thing I love is Cassie," Beck said, her voice steady. "And you don't get to have her anymore. Now get the hell out of here, or we'll call the cops. Again."

"You know what?" Nico spat, throwing his arms in the air. "Not worth my time."

He looked up to the window then, right at Cassie, and raised his voice again. "Hear that, Cassie? You're not worth it, baby!"

Then he got into his car and sped down the road.

When Beck came back upstairs, they all climbed into bed. The combination of the alcohol the night before, stress, and sleeplessness, and then the sharp spike of fear, had worn them out all over again. So they slept. Well past noon, far into New Year's Day. Then they made coffee in Beck's kitchen, and drank it sitting on the porch. They tried to salvage the day with painted nails and music, and discussing absolutely nothing of significance, because everything of significance hurt too much. Grandpa. Nico. Cassie.

Beck kept the baseball bat with her the entire weekend, and then in the van. As though that was enough. As though it was all she needed to take down Nico Bell if he reared his ugly, violent head again. Nico Bell, with his anger and his guns and an entire town eating out of the palm of his hand.

Vivian wished it had been true.

Vivian wished their love had been enough to keep Cassie safe.

* * *

Vivian and Beck let Merit take notes as they described what happened. She was focused in on the details of the New Year's Eve incident, laying it out as a timeline of events.

When did they leave the party? What time did they arrive at the police station?

Did Cassie have any paperwork from the police? Was there a police report?

When did Nico arrive the next morning?

Vivian thought carefully and answered what she could. There were a few questions they didn't know the answers to, though Cassie would.

But Vivian couldn't exactly explain that they'd have to consult with their ghost and get back to her, so she just said she'd try to remember if Cassie ever said anything else.

"Did either of you know that there is a domestic violence clinic a half hour from here?" Merit asked, finally setting her pen down.

"No," Beck said, and Vivian shrugged.

"The Bell police have worked with them for years. They bring in advocates to support victims of domestic violence, sexual assault. Cassie never mentioned them?"

"No, I don't think she ever went to them," Vivian told her. "We would have been the ones to take her, probably."

"You don't have to go to them," Merit said. "The police call them, bring them in when there's a case related to their work. Cassie never mentioned them?"

"She didn't. She had a few pamphlets when we left the station that night. Maybe one of those . . . ?" Vivian trailed off when Merit shook her head.

"It should have been a phone call. An advocate would have personally come to be with Cassie for those interviews. Would have helped Cassie with a protection order."

Beck shook her head. "That never happened."

"Okay, thanks," Merit said. "I know this sucks to talk about. I really appreciate your time."

"Whatever we can do," Vivian answered.

She liked Merit. She'd liked the show, too, even before meeting her in person. It was honest, and she didn't shy away from calling out bad men by name when it was warranted.

And it was warranted a lot, Vivian was learning.

"One last question," Merit said, leaning forward. "But it's important. When Cassie was in the hospital in March, when she did finally get that protection order, the hospital recorded two visitors to her room that evening. I know one of them was Sheriff Thomas. But the other is just a scribble on the form, and the hospital won't give me access to the security tapes. Do you know who went with the sheriff to Cassie's room that day? Could it have been an advocate from the clinic?"

That question Vivian could answer.

Cassie never told them when she was alive, but when

they asked for the entire awful story, she'd talked about the day she filed for a protection order. The day she went to the hospital.

Vivian only knew what happened next because Cassie, only mostly dead and haunting Beck's van, had been able to tell them.

"That wasn't a victim services advocate," Vivian said. "It was Bell."

"Nico Bell was allowed into that hospital?" Merit said.

"Not Nico. His father. Steven Bell."

Merit's face turned to stone at the words, her lips trembling with anger before they formed a hard, straight line. Vivian knew that look well. She knew the anger that shaped it. If someone had asked Vivian six months ago, she wouldn't have recognized it. But now she knew it felt like a worm, dug deep into her. It filled her with things she never asked for—grief and loss, and the feeling of powerlessness that had frozen her since March. She'd wondered if it would be there always now, something she'd have to draw from, and looking at Merit, she thought, *Yes*, this she'd have to carry. She didn't ask for this anger, but here it was, part of her, the same as her scarred leg, the same as her scarred heart, which she knew would long for Cassie after she left them for good. Vivian wished she could dig it out of herself, like the parasite it was, but it was rooted too deep. Tugging it out would only hurt her more. Some things you have to take

247

with you, and hope you'll get used to the weight of them.

"Okay," Merit said. "I have everything I need to move forward. Thank you. Really, thank you for agreeing to talk to me. I know it's not easy to trust anyone right now."

Merit stood, began packing up her things.

"Wait," Vivian said. "I have a question for you."

Merit waited.

"Why are you here, really?"

"Why do you think?" Merit asked, a sad twist of a smile on her face. "I'm back here for the same reason neither of you can leave yet. Vengeance."

"Vengeance against who, Merit?" Vivian asked.

"The Bells," she said. "They aren't going to get away with hurting girls anymore."

WE CAN BE HEROES
SEASON 2: EPISODE 18
"THE ADVOCATE"

MERIT LOGAN: Welcome back to We Can Be Heroes, *listeners. In the United States, women are twenty-one times more likely to be killed by a gun than women in peer countries. Firearm access and intimate-partner violence converge violently in the US, where on average, fifty-three women are shot and killed by an intimate partner every month. To gain a little insight into the work behind this data, and what direct service agencies do to address it, I've invited Margaret Swift, director of the local domestic violence clinic, Sarah's Place.*

MERIT: Welcome, Dr. Swift.

DR. SWIFT: Thank you, Merit.

MERIT: Tell me about your organization.

DR. SWIFT: Sarah's Place was founded in the mid-1980s. There was a major shift in the decade prior concerning domestic violence—but it took a long time for the laws to catch up with what women knew was going on. In the meantime, a lot of shelters started in homes, providing survivors a place to sleep that was safe. Sarah's Place is named after the founder's daughter, who was murdered in 1983 by her husband.

MERIT: Do you see that a lot in victim advocacy? People

getting involved in activism for personal reasons, or to honor victims they knew?

DR. SWIFT: Absolutely. Unfortunately, it often takes that personal tie-in for people to become aware of how devastating the impact of intimate-partner violence is, and to see how those situations can turn quickly from uncomfortable to fatal.

MERIT: Have you been following what's happening with the murals in Bell?

DR. SWIFT: I have. We've watched the story gain some traction, some notice from our congresswoman, for one.

MERIT: Do you have any thoughts on it?

DR. SWIFT: Only to say that it feels in line with the work we do at the clinic. The spirit of it, at least.

MERIT: How so?

DR. SWIFT: Well, those women who took others into their own homes in the seventies? They were going against society and the law, helping women leave their husbands at a time when marital rape and abuse wasn't even considered illegal in many places. Sometimes what's legal and what's right aren't the same thing.

MERIT: Does your clinic work with the Bell Police Department?

DR. SWIFT: We have a close working relationship. We provide annual training on violence for their officers. They call us in for domestic violence cases, filing protection orders, victim compensation services . . . things like that.

MERIT: Was your agency contacted about Cassie Queen?

DR. SWIFT: No, we were not.

MERIT: Dr. Swift, how often does Bell contact your clinic for help with their cases?

DR. SWIFT: I thought you might ask this, so I pulled our statistics for the county, and for the town of Bell.

MERIT: I pulled that data for the town, too.

DR. SWIFT: And you saw that there were nineteen temporary protection order requests filed in Bell last year?

MERIT: Every one of them included the request to temporarily relinquish firearms.

DR. SWIFT: We try to always include that, and advocates from our organization assisted with all those requests.

MERIT: You were contacted for every single one?

DR. SWIFT: Last year, yes.

MERIT: Tell me about your training program for the officers. They understand the seriousness of domestic violence . . . the potential danger?

DR. SWIFT: Of course. For their safety, too. Domestic calls are some of the most dangerous that police respond to.

MERIT: What about teen dating violence? Did you discuss that, too?

DR. SWIFT: We did. But only to say that, pattern wise, it looks very similar to what we see with married or dating adults. The ages don't matter, so much as the risk factors.

That's why we recommend all officers screen for lethality.

MERIT: Can you explain that further?

DR. SWIFT: A lethality screening is a series of questions that we encourage officers and advocates to ask to determine the severity of the case—meaning the likelihood that a fatality could occur without meaningful intervention.

MERIT: What kind of questions are in that screening?

DR. SWIFT: Well, threats to kill, threats using a weapon, access to a gun—

MERIT: Sorry, excuse me, but access to a gun specifically is one of the questions?

DR. SWIFT: Yes.

MERIT: Why is that?

DR. SWIFT: Studies show that access to a firearm makes it five times more likely that a woman will be killed by an abusive partner.

MERIT: If Cassie had been referred to an advocate, would they have gone through a lethality screening with her? Would Nico's access to guns have been a red flag?

DR. SWIFT: Undoubtedly. We can never predict which cases will become as severe as Cassie's did, but the history of violence, the way it was escalating, and Nico's access to firearms all would have led us to believe that Cassie was in danger.

CASSIE

I was crying before
we got off the stage
our last performance
March of senior year.

It felt like grief—
leaving that stage behind.
Like some part of me knew
it'd be the last time I'd sing.

The whole drama club
gathered backstage
half-undressed, hurrying,
eager to go, to celebrate.

I was fresh-faced and out of there
in about seven minutes flat.

They were waiting for me.
Beck, Vivian, Betty,
and the lake in March,
a horrible,
freezing thing.
But it was tradition.

When I rounded the corner,
he was waiting for me.

Matteo,
holding sunflowers.
Brilliant gold splashes
in the drab hallway.

It was new. That us.
It had only been weeks.
Weeks of gentle words,
weeks of gentle touches,
a hand graze in the hall.
We kept it quiet,
because it was new,
and because I didn't know
if he was still watching me.

The texts had finally stopped.
The I want you back texts,

the How dare you leave me *texts,*
the I can't believe you
went to the police
are you trying
to ruin
my life
texts.

We'd kept our secret,
but there was no one left backstage,
so when Matteo leaned in
and kissed me
in a spot that might
be called my cheek
but was also the edge
of my smile,
I turned into it
and caught him full-on.

I kissed him
like I'd wanted to
like I wasn't scared anymore,
and it was sweet.
He was sweet.
But in a moment,
Matteo was gone,
thrown against the lockers

and it was Nico there
in his place,
towering over me,
red-faced, and when he spoke
he was so angry that flecks of spit
hit my face and neck
and when I backed away
he followed
his hand finding my shoulder
sliding up to my neck,
squeezing.

I heard Matteo's shout,
and felt when he slammed into Nico,
who released me, gasping.
He called me a name,
before turning and leaving.
Walking away.
Like he had no reason to hurry.
No reason to worry.
I hit the floor sobbing,
and Matteo held me,
until Vivian and Beck
came looking for me.
And then their arms
took over for him.

Vivian talked to me
in hushed, urgent whispers,
We've got you.
We've got you now.

Beck's anger was quiet.
But sometimes quiet
is a violent thing, too.

BECK

BECK TRIPPED OVER A PAIR OF legs on the porch as she tried to sneak in.

"What the—"

"Language," came a gruff voice from the rocking chair. Beck hadn't even seen him there.

"Grandpa. It's two o'clock in the morning. What are you doing out here?"

Her grandfather sat up in the chair, looking around the dark porch. "Did you say two? Why are you leaving at two in the morning?"

"I'm *not* leaving," Beck said. "I'm coming back."

"I've been out here since ten," he said with a soft laugh, standing up and stretching. "I wanted to catch you sneaking out after you said no more murals for a while." Grandpa rested his hand on the top of Beck's head as he spoke, a gesture he'd always done in affection.

"Well, you did catch me," she said. "You caught me getting

home, Grandpa. I left the house early tonight, around sunset."

"Sunset?" he repeated. "I must have not realized. Just assumed you were upstairs painting. Didn't see Betty."

"She was over by the field," Beck said. "I've been parking over there the last few weeks."

"Right, right," Grandpa said. "Were you painting?"

Beck dropped her gaze, unable to lie to him, but unable to tell him she went back on her word.

"All right, Beck. It's all right. Well, like I said before, you are an adult. You get to make your own choices. But Bell is a powerful man. If he thinks what you're doing will hurt his company, he'll come after you hard."

"I don't want to hurt his company," Beck said. "I want to destroy it."

Grandpa shuffled over and held the screen door for Beck.

"Things'll get ugly in town," he warned. "And Cassie is gone."

"She's not *gone*," Beck said. "I mean. I *feel* like she's still here. I feel like I have to fight for her. And things are already ugly."

Grandpa didn't argue with Beck any more. He nodded his understanding, squeezed her shoulder. He said a soft good night at the stairs. "Be careful."

Beck sat up for hours in her window, her eyes fixed on the van across the yard.

Her eyes fixed on Cassie standing next to the van.

259

She looked almost alive.

That blue glow of hers could be mistaken for moonlight on her face. But Beck knew better. She knew Cassie wasn't alive. No matter how she wished it. And she knew Cassie was almost ready to go.

Beck slept terribly, plagued by nightmares. Rather, one nightmare, on repeat, again and again. A familiar one. She dreamed she was in that classroom that day. Dreamed it was her leg ruined, her body next to Cassie. She dreamed it over and over, and each time, she tried to move fast enough. She tried to stop him, or at least get in front of Cass before the first shot rang out across the desks. But she was never fast enough. That moment in the classroom wasn't the moment that anyone could have saved Cassie. The chance to save her had come earlier, with the police. At the hospital. When Cassie had asked for help.

So Beck slept terribly, and in the morning she woke with more guilt than the day before.

She would never blame Vivian for not saving Cassie.

Why couldn't she stop blaming herself?

It wasn't quite sunset the following evening when Beck's phone started to buzz in her pocket. She was elbow-deep in an engine, covered in oil and grime.

"Shit," she said.

She cleaned off quickly and checked her messages. A

voice mail from an unknown number.

Beck, this is Merit. Merit Logan. I got a call from a friend of mine. The police just brought in some kid for questioning about the murals? I guess he got caught posting to the social media account for the murals, over at the Tannersville library.

Shit. Matteo was in trouble.

The kid's name is . . . Matteo. Do you know him? Is he helping you? My friend says as far as she knows he was not arrested. The police just asked him to come in and talk to them, but, Beck, he could be in serious trouble if they can link him to the murals in some way. I'm on my way over there now. Maybe you and Vivian can meet me in the town square? I'll try to get him out of there.

Beck ran for the van, shouting a quick goodbye to Grandpa through the kitchen window. She called Vivian, who had just talked to Merit and was already on her way.

Beck didn't know what to expect in town, but it wasn't the scene that greeted her as she parked Betty. The sun was slipping over the horizon, and Cassie appeared in the passenger seat, but she was quiet, taking in the scene.

There were people filling the town square, shouting, carrying signs.

"What the hell?" Beck asked, jumping at a rapping sound on her driver's side window.

Vivian.

"Cass, we'll be back as soon as we can."

Beck didn't wait for Cassie to answer. She was out and moving with Vivian toward the crowd. On the edge was Lola Talbot. She was holding a sign.

FUCK BELL GUNS.

"Lola," Vivian said, reaching for Lola's arm. "Lola, what is this?"

"Hey, glad you two made it," Lola said, hugging them both.

"Made what?" Beck asked. She started to recognize more people in the crowd. Friends from school. Some teachers, too. "When did this start?"

"Just an hour ago," Lola said. "I've been following Merit's podcast—and her social media. When I realized it was Matteo they brought in, I called the drama club, and they called the chorus club, who called debate, who called the teachers' phone line, and . . . well, everyone wanted to show up. For Cassie. For Matteo. They're questioning him over *nothing*. All he did was post the photos online. And he did it for Cassie. This is bullshit."

Beck started reading the signs around them.

Gun Control Now.

For Cassie.

Bell Guns KILL.

Protect Our Girls.

"These people are all here . . . in support of Cassie?"

"Not all," Lola said, gesturing to a group on the other side of Town Hall. They didn't have signs. And they were silent. But they were all armed. "They say they're here to protect the peace."

"They're here for Bell," Vivian said, her eyes going dark with anger.

Then the door to the police station opened, and Merit Logan was walking down the steps with Matteo. Everyone surrounding Beck started to cheer, and across the town square, the others began to yell.

Matteo made eye contact with Beck over the crowd, lifted his hand in a jerky wave.

"He sees us," Beck told Vivian. "We need to get out of here."

Matteo made his way through the crowd, but he was stopped often by people telling him to keep going. To keep talking about Cassie. How much they missed her. Beck wanted to stop and appreciate this—this outpouring of love. Of acknowledgment.

But there wasn't any time. Beck turned to say something to Vivian, but she wasn't there.

Beck scanned the town square, searching for her, and finally spotted her near the gazebo. What was Vivian doing? She could just barely see her, walking right toward the other group—the armed group. Then Vivian dropped out of sight.

When she finally broke through the crowd, Beck found Vivian heading right for one of the armed men, the look in her eyes wild and far away.

She was being reckless.

Beck grabbed for her, pulling her back and down.

"Vivian. Vivian, you can't start anything with them. *Vivian.*"

One of the armed men had a loudspeaker and was addressing the rest of them.

Beck only caught the tail end of his words. ". . . all because a good kid made one bad choice."

At first Beck thought he meant Cassie, and she felt a surge of anger that he would blame *her* for any part of it. And then she realized. *A good kid.*

They were talking about *Nico.*

Beck turned, thinking she would need to physically restrain Vivian from going after that man, but Vivian had frozen next to Beck, her eyes trained on the man closest to them—on his gun. Beck watched as Vivian's face turned ashen, and she started to shake. Suddenly her legs buckled, and Vivian was kneeling on the ground.

That's where Matteo found them.

He knelt beside Vivian, one hand finding her pulse on her wrist, the other gently tipping up her face to look at her eyes.

"I think she's having a panic attack, Beck. We really need to get her out of here."

Beck and Matteo worked together, getting Vivian onto her feet and each wrapping an arm around her middle. They made their way around the crowd this time, instead of through it.

Down the street, back to Betty. Back to safety.

There was a shout behind her, and Beck turned.

The gazebo was on fire—Beck could see the flames climbing fast against the dark sky. Heard a siren start to wail in the distance from the fire hall.

It was chaos.

They finally made it to the block where Betty was parked, and Beck stopped short.

She saw Cassie, once again beside the van instead of inside it. And in front of her, facing a store window, was Steven Bell.

Beck watched as Mr. Bell looked at his reflection in the glass window of the gun shop. A streetlamp flickered on. He straightened his tie, and the smug smile curling on his face made Beck sick to look at him, but she couldn't tear her eyes away as Mr. Bell's gaze shifted, so slightly, to the reflection beside his own.

To Cassie.

Cassie met his gaze, for a moment, then reached down to the bricks circling a tree on the sidewalk. Cassie's fingers sunk into the dirt, and Beck watched as she wrapped her hand around the brick, watched her lift the heaviness of it as she stood, arching her arm back over her head.

Cassie threw it at Bell.

The brick hit the storefront window right in front of him, shattering it. A million little shards came down, looking like stars glimmering in the night sky as they fell down in the dark.

Mr. Bell threw his arms up to shield his face.

While he was too distracted to notice them, Beck herded her friends into the van. She had to save them now, the ones she loved most: a broken girl, an earnest boy, and a rightfully vengeful ghost.

CASSIE

Bell is on fire.

I recognize my neighbors
clashing in the town square.

I see Principal Ewing,
who once told me I'd be a star,
now standing with a sign
demanding Bell Firearms
take responsibility
for my death.

There's the Warren family,
whose sunflowers shape
the festival each year,
calling for the sheriff's
removal.

On their sign
is the image of Cassandra
from Beck's first mural.
For Cassie,
it says along
the bottom.

They've brought
their children,
who I used to babysit.

Protect Our Girls
from Their Abusers,
reads another sign.
The mother holding it
has a baby strapped
to her chest.
Imagine feeling
the urgency,
the fear,
to start protesting for
your baby girl
before she's old enough
to walk.

Children Not Guns,

says another sign.
Gun Control Now.

Fuck Bell Guns.

That sign is held by Lola.
Lola, my friend.
Lola, who saw me die.

But that is only one side
of the gathered crowd
on this warm August
evening.

The other side looks different.
They don't look angrier, exactly.
Meaner, perhaps.
And they are armed
to the teeth.

I'm out of the van
but can't go farther.
When I try to take a step
toward the courthouse,
toward Beck, Vivian, Matteo,
it's like pins and needles, and

then nothingness.
Like I'm slipping away
from them a little more
with each step I take
to get closer.

So I wait by the van,
furious and terrified,
because I don't see
how the mothers cradling
their babies
and teenagers barely
out of high school
can stand up to
all these angry men
and all their guns.

Movement catches my eye
from the sidewalk
and I turn.

Steven Bell is standing
right behind me,
looking through me,
at the crowd.

There is a faint smile
on his lips.
Like he knows
which side has the power.

The last time I saw Mr. Bell
was two days before I died.

Instead of jumping in
the lake, I went to the hospital
for the bruising
on my neck,
my strained voice,
my scratchy vocal cords.

When the hospital reported
my injuries to the police,
they sent the sheriff.

And the sheriff
brought Mr. Bell.

I remember feeling
like nothing at all.
Like gum on the bottom
of his shoe

when he walked
right into my hospital room
like he owned everything—
because he did.
He owned the town
and still does now.

He told me Nico
would stay away from me
this time.
He would take care of it.
But would I consider,
in exchange,
not filing a police report.

Think of his future,
Mr. Bell said to me,
and the sheriff let him say it.
He said Nico would stay home,
finish high school online,
so he wasn't kicked out.
That way he could still swim.

He said it like it was
the swimming
that mattered most

more than the bruises
in the shape of Nico's hand
on my neck.

It hurt to talk.
It hurt to tell him:
No
but I said no
to Mr. Bell that day.

I'm filing a report,
I told them,
looking right at the sheriff.
And I want a protection order.
And I want Nico
out of school, completely.
Or I want him arrested.

Mr. Bell looked like maybe
he'd like to try
to strangle me, too.
Instead he stormed out.

The sheriff had to
let me file, but
when it came to the part

about removing guns from
the abuser's house,
he scoffed, and said,
We can't do that to the Bells.
It's their legacy. Besides,
they probably
outgun the department.

But Nico didn't care
about his family's legacy
or about swim team.
Nico cared only
about possession.

He had always been
a spoiled child
and he became
a jealous man.
An angry man
with access to an
arsenal in his house.
So the only decision
Nico had to make
was which gun to use
to make sure I never sang
for anyone but him again.

I turn and
face the glass storefront,
and Mr. Bell
turns as well.

Betty the van was parked,
ironically,
outside of the Bell gun shop
on Main Street.

Mr. Bell straightens his tie
in his reflection
but then he looks up
and his eyes find mine
in the window
and I think, He sees me.
He sees *me*.

Bell looks like he's seen a ghost—
probably because he has.
His face goes pale,
and his hand lowers slowly to his side.

When I reach for the brick
half-buried in the flower bed
at my feet

I don't actually know
if I can lift it.

This is harder than pressing
a button on a phone,
or honking a horn,
but I wrap my hand around it.

I am stronger now.

When I grasp it,
I don't hesitate.
I rise, and I hurl it
as hard as I can
at the glass.

I have watched
my friends rage for weeks now,
their anger behind everything they do
and it's my anger, too.
It's my life that the Bells stole.

And it'll happen again
today or tomorrow
in this town,
or the next.
Another girl.

And then her friends
will be left to wonder
what the currency of vengeance is
in a world that tells girls
we shouldn't be angry,
even as our lives
are ripped
from our grasps.

When I throw the brick,
I picture myself
as a small child,
throwing pennies in a pond
making wishes.

So tonight I wish, too,
and the wish begins
If only—

If only this world loved living girls
as much as it loves dead ones.

VIVIAN

THEY PARKED BETTY BY THE SUNFLOWER field.

Vivian was breathing normally again, following Matteo's directions. It wasn't the first panic attack, and she doubted it would be the last.

"How long have you been getting them?" Matteo asked gently.

"I don't know," Vivian said.

"Yes, you do," Matteo insisted.

Vivian was watching Beck. Her grip on the steering wheel was so tight her knuckles were white.

"Beck?" she asked.

"Are you . . . are you guys okay? If I go? There's something I need to do." Beck's voice was thick with the weight of unshed tears.

"I got her from here," Matteo said. "I'll drive her home."

"Okay," Beck said. "Bye, V. Bye, Ca—" Beck stopped short, and her eyes found Vivian's in the rearview mirror.

Vivian was sitting right next to Cassie, but Matteo didn't see her.

"Bye, Matteo," Beck finished, and climbed out of the van.

Vivian and Matteo climbed out next, and Vivian gave Cassie a warm smile, and a shrug, before shutting the van door. She couldn't exactly talk to her in front of Matteo. A conversation about Bell and the brick and the town square would have to wait.

They walked to Vivian's car and Matteo held out his hands for her keys.

"So are you in trouble?" Vivian asked.

"Nah, don't worry about it," Matteo said. He dismissed it too easily.

"Matteo," Vivian said, collapsing into the passenger seat. "Tell me."

"Someone saw me posting on the library computer. Called the cops. I think he thought he'd get Bell's fancy reward or something. But all I was doing was exercising my rights to free speech, so they can't do anything unless they can link me to the murals themselves. And they can't. Merit helped. She's cool."

"Yeah, she is."

"I thought we hated Bell, but wow."

"Right?" Vivian said. "She's out for blood."

"Good," Matteo said.

Matteo opened his mouth several times as he drove,

and then closed it again.

Vivian stopped waiting for it—she knew what he wanted to say. He was going to tell them to stop what they were doing. But they couldn't stop, not yet. Cassie was still here. She still needed them to fight for her.

"Son of a bitch," Vivian said when she saw the water tower. "Matteo, pull over."

Matteo stopped the car along the side of the road and leaned over to Vivian's side.

Vivian pointed.

The water tower mural was gone.

In its place was a sunflower, and the words *ANNUAL BELL SUNFLOWER FESTIVAL* with the dates for next week.

They had *literally* covered up Cassie with the festival.

It was starting to feel a little desperate to Vivian. They were aggressively trying to gloss over the hurt in town, trying to make it look peaceful and inviting to the outside world. And the reality couldn't be further from the truth, with everyone clashing in the town square, armed with guns, armed with nothing but their signs and a plea for safety.

"Can we . . . can we please check the others?" Vivian asked.

She was feeling defeated. All that work was gone.

"Sure thing," Matteo said. He drove them around town, to the billboard on Route 90, now covered with more flowers, and a little map showing how to get to the fields by the Warrens' farm, where the festival would take place.

They checked the high school next—no advertisement there, and no red paint, either, but the mural was painted over with the school's mascot.

Last they drove to the Old Mill. They hadn't even gotten a picture of it—had they really just finished painting it the night before? It felt like so long ago.

Vivian let out a huge sigh of relief to see it was still there. They probably hadn't found it yet.

"Just a sec," she told Matteo, climbing out of the car. Matteo had parked with the headlights illuminating Circe and her island. It wouldn't be a great photo, taken in the dark like this, but Vivian couldn't wait. They might paint over it by tomorrow.

They for sure wouldn't leave it up until the festival.

Wouldn't want to mar Bell's image.

She took a few photos while she still could.

As soon as she was back in the car, Matteo drove them both home. He parked outside their shared row of houses.

Vivian knew he had something to say. She'd spent enough time with him to know. Matteo had always been the quiet type, but when he did speak up, she listened. So she waited.

She opened the account she'd made for Cassie, the one Matteo had taken over for the last two murals. She scrolled up to the original post. *Cassandra* was going viral this week—there were millions of likes. The others had gained traction, too, but not as much as the original one.

The one that shared Cassie's name.

Vivian followed the links, reading the comments. It was a lot of teens, angry about the active-shooter drills in school. Angry that their little sister or cousin or best friend hadn't been able to enforce a protection order because it would have forced their abuser out of school.

Furious that they couldn't keep themselves safe. Each other safe.

#FuckBellGuns was trending. When Vivian clicked on the tag, the top image was from the town square tonight. Lola was standing there with her sign, and in the background of the image, only slightly hazy, you could make out the armed men behind her.

Vivian squeezed Matteo's hand.

Their friends were so brave. Matteo got pulled in by the cops. Lola didn't back down from those men. And Merit Logan seemed hell-bent on exposing the truth.

All wasn't lost just because they'd destroyed the murals.

"Vivian . . . I think it's time to stop," Matteo finally said. "I know that you and Beck are trying to keep Cassie's memory alive—trying to fight for some real change, in her memory, and I think that's really amazing, but this? This is getting dangerous. You could get hurt. You're definitely gonna get caught eventually. And then you lose college, and—"

"I already told you I'm not going," she said.

"Dammit, Vivian. Listen to yourself. You can't give up

everything you worked so hard for just because—"

"*Just because* what, Matteo? Cassie was murdered. I think the adults who were supposed to protect her should face some responsibility."

"I was going to say, just because of one asshole. Screw Nico Bell. He already stole Cassie's future. Why should he get yours, too?"

Vivian sat with his words for a long moment, turning them over in her mind. The logical part of Vivian—the part that used to rule every choice she made—knew he was right. The thing was, even now, it was worth the risk for Cassie. She had to think of Cassie.

"We aren't done yet," Vivian said quietly, and Matteo swore under his breath and turned away from her.

"Well, I'm out," Matteo said. "My name's all over this now. My mom's probably going to get fired because of it—and I know"—he raised his hands—"that's on me, not you, V. I took that risk. But I thought it'd be enough now. I thought if I helped you and Beck, it would be enough."

"Well, it's not."

"Vivian, you did it. Everyone is talking about Cass. The gun lobby is losing their minds, let alone Bell himself, setting up a reward to catch you. Let Merit take over from here. Stop breaking the law before you get caught. And call your fancy college and tell them you are coming. You can do it. You just need to ask for a little help, V. You know this gets better. You *know* it does."

"Thank you, Matteo. For helping with the posts," Vivian said. "I know getting pulled in by the police must have been kind of scary."

"Vivian—"

"We can't stop yet, Matteo. We aren't finished."

"Vivian, the lawsuit will take years," Matteo said. "Let justice find a way in the courts. You and Beck are playing with fire here."

"You don't understand. We *cannot* stop, because we have to help her."

"Help who?" Matteo asked.

"Cassie," Vivian said. There was only one way to make Matteo understand why they couldn't stop yet. She had to tell him the truth. "Matteo, we can't stop. Because Cassie's still here."

"What the hell are you talking about?"

"Cassie has been haunting the hell out of us."

BECK

BECK KNEW WHERE HE KEPT THEM.

She pushed open the heavy door to Grandpa's workshop
and tugged on the string for the swinging light bulb over his
bench. It was eerie in the workshop at night, full of shadows
and the scurrying sounds of mice in the rafters.

But Beck knew she wouldn't be able to rest until she did
this.

She knew where he kept them, and she knew where the
combination lock was written down. Four numbers written
on the corner of his desk. Her mother's birthday. That's what
the numbers were. Grandpa used it for every password,
even though she'd told him countless times that wasn't safe.

She went for the cabinet next, punched in the numbers
and let the door swing wide. Beck vaguely wondered if it
had been this easy for Nico that day. Maybe even easier.

Grandpa owned five guns. Two rifles that he used to
hunt with, back when he still hunted. And three handguns

that Beck imagined had been locked away in this safe for a decade or more. But their lack of use didn't change what they were capable of.

She started with a rifle and a hammer.

She swung it as hard as she could, but missed the first time, her vision blurry with tears that she kept pausing to wipe away furiously.

She swung again, and it marked the smooth metal side. But it was just a scrape, a ding. It wasn't enough. Beck got up again, heading for the back room, where Grandpa stored things they didn't need as often. She reached for the sledgehammer that they used to tear down a wall years ago.

She started swinging again, this time with both hands wrapped around it, putting all her force behind the movement. This time, she aimed for the name on the gun, etched into its side. Bell Firearms.

Beck swung hard.

A dent appeared.

Then two, three. The barrel of the rifle caved in, but only slightly.

It still wasn't *enough*. Beck wanted them in pieces. She wanted them to be nothing.

If Cassie's body could be reduced to dirt and ash, then goddammit, the guns would be, too.

She lifted the rifle and carried it to the vise grip mounted on the workbench. She tossed the weapon in and twisted the lever until it was tight. Then she reached for the sledge-hammer again and aimed for the handle.

This time she broke off a chunk, splintering the wood. She swung again, and again, and again.

She hit the rifle as hard as she could, but the sledgeham-mer was heavy, and her arms were burning, and she felt it in her chest, the heaviness of it all. Losing Cass, fighting for her now. Watching their town turn against them just for wanting that loss to not be in vain. Watching them choose that company, again and again. All of it hit Beck as she swung that hammer, and it hurt, *it hurt*.

Suddenly the sledgehammer weighed nothing at all.

It had been pulled from her hands, and Beck let it go, collapsing on the oil-stained concrete floor of the garage, sobbing. Beck felt her chest heaving, trying to suck in air.

But Grandpa was right there. He set the sledgehammer down and knelt beside her on the floor. He held her. Wrapped her up tight in his arms, grounding her to the earth, to this life she still had.

Beck sobbed until there was nothing left in her. But Grandpa stayed.

When she finally lifted her head, she was dizzy, exhausted. This day was never-ending.

Grandpa helped her stand up.

"It's too much for anyone's shoulders, honey," Grandpa said. "You've been so strong. But this . . ." He gestured to the dented rifle, the abandoned sledgehammer. "This isn't going to work."

Beck nodded. He was right. Destroying five guns wouldn't change anything. Wouldn't bring Cassie back, not really. Wouldn't help her move on, either. It didn't mean anything, except for what it meant to Beck.

But then Grandpa reached for one of the handguns in the cabinet and put it in a long metal bin that he'd pulled out from under his bench. He went to his tool cabinet next and came back with a blowtorch.

Beck sat on the stool. *This isn't going to work*, he'd said, staring at the sledgehammer.

Beck watched her grandpa turn on the torch. He cut through the handgun, moving slowly. He sliced through the metal, diagonally, and then went back and held the blowtorch in place, sealing off the severed ends, turning barrels and mechanisms into solid blocks of metal. The gun was beyond repair. It would never fire a bullet again.

When he was done with that one, he reached for the rifle Beck had been working on. He gestured for Beck and handed her the blowtorch and a pair of goggles.

He showed her where to cut. Diagonal lines at crucial places, to ensure that it was incapacitated forever.

Beck destroyed them all, one by one. She finished and turned the blowtorch off, dropped the goggles onto the bench. Grandpa put his arm around her, staring down into the bin that now contained nothing but scraps of metal.

"Good work, Beck," he said, holding tight. "Proud of you, honey."

Beck cried again, leaning into his arm, grateful that he understood. Grateful that she wasn't alone. Grateful to be part of his universe, right here on earth. Home.

WE CAN BE HEROES
SEASON 2: EPISODE 19
"THE SHERIFF"

[Phone recording]

MERIT LOGAN: Sheriff Thomas, I'm surprised to hear from you again.

SHERIFF THOMAS: I imagine you are, Ms. Logan. You've been creating quite a stir around here. Interrogating everyone from our deputies to the editor of the paper.

MERIT: I'm letting you know that I'm recording this call.

SHERIFF THOMAS: That's fine, Ms. Logan. We've got nothing to hide. Listen, we're all heartbroken over what happened to Ms. Queen in March. But you are looking for fault in what was simply a tragedy. Sometimes tragedies can't be avoided.

MERIT: . . . Sometimes they can.

SHERIFF THOMAS: Well, we've got a lot of angry people in town. They're saying you're the one pushing the murals to the top of the news cycle. You're supporting that lawsuit. You've got an agenda. Now we have protests happening right in our town square. Maybe it's time to move along and ruin another town.

[Soft laughter]

MERIT: Well, I'm not completely done with this one yet. Sheriff, before you go, I do have one last question for you . . . why wasn't the domestic violence clinic called in for Cassie?

SHERIFF THOMAS: It just wasn't that serious a case—it didn't—it didn't seem that serious.

MERIT: You didn't think Nico maybe shouldn't have access to guns?

SHERIFF THOMAS: That would have been an extreme response, I think, Ms. Logan.

MERIT: Sir, were you required to attend the domestic violence trainings run by Dr. Swift from Sarah's Place?

SHERIFF THOMAS: I wasn't required. I chose to attend.

MERIT: Did Dr. Swift explain to you why the lethality assessment asks about choking, specifically?

SHERIFF THOMAS: Oh, I can't recall.

MERIT: It's because choking, or an attempt to strangle someone, is very often the penultimate act to a fatality.

SHERIFF THOMAS: That's right.

MERIT: Sir, can you remind me what Cassie's injuries were the day you visited her in the hospital?

SHERIFF THOMAS: She had some bruising, on her arms, her shoulder . . .

MERIT: And her throat. I've seen the pictures, Sheriff. And the hospital notes. Nico choked Cassie that day.

SHERIFF THOMAS: He did, but we didn't think—

MERIT: Sheriff, who went with you that day, to the hospital?

SHERIFF THOMAS: Excuse me?

MERIT: There is a visitor log. Someone signed in with you, but it's illegible. Who was with you that day?

SHERIFF THOMAS: I don't recall. Probably Deputy Everett.

MERIT: No, he wasn't there. I've already spoken with him.

SHERIFF THOMAS: Ms. Logan, I've got a job to get back to now.

MERIT: Very well, Sheriff Thomas. One last question.

SHERIFF THOMAS: All right.

MERIT: There was another lawsuit filed against Steven Bell eight years ago, and then withdrawn. It was a civil suit, for personal damages. Do you recall that? You were a brand-new sheriff that year.

SHERIFF THOMAS: I do not.

MERIT: The lawsuit alleged that Mr. Bell took advantage of a young woman—an intern with the mayor's office. It said that Bell had "special access" to the mayor and used that access to lure this young woman into an affair. He would have been forty-four years old at the time. The young woman was seventeen.

SHERIFF THOMAS: Oh, that. That was nonsense. It was all consensual. Inconsequential.

[Extended silence]

MERIT: It may seem inconsequential, but it may well come up now that Mr. Bell is facing yet another lawsuit. What happened to the young woman?

SHERIFF THOMAS: That girl was trying to make a name

for herself. It ended up not being the kind of name she wanted. Bell residents turned on her fast. Last I heard, she moved to another state. Probably to try to start fresh. She went away.

MERIT: You mean the problem went away.

SHERIFF THOMAS: As far as we were concerned, that was the same thing.

MERIT: Did you feel that way about Cassie Queen, too?

[Phone call disconnects]

MERIT LOGAN: Well, listeners, we seem to have lost our connection. Okay, well, this is a long shot, but here it goes. I want to talk to Steven Bell. Mr. Bell, I doubt you're listening, but I know your people are. So here it is: an invitation for you to come on my podcast. You get to tell your side of the story. Tell us what happened to Cassie Queen. I promise I don't bite, Mr. Bell.

MURAL 6

TITLE: HELEN

LOCATION: BELL LAKE LEVEE

CASSIE

Beck's grandpa dies
with a smile on his lips
a cheek full of tobacco
and the sun shining
on his face.

Beck had said
that they were luckier
than most,
they'd had time to talk
about his last wishes,
all those strange
end-of-life details
that don't mean anything
until they mean everything.

They had already talked
about his funeral:

No.
And his burial:
At St. Mary's
next to my wife.
And even the precise
wording of his
obituary:
You just tell
Jack O'Day
that he wins the bet
but I'm not paying him.

He dies on the porch
while Beck works in
his mechanic shop
and at first when she returns,
she thinks he's asleep.

It is the day of the
Bell Sunflower Festival
and tonight is when
Vivian and Beck planned
to do the next mural
in the most visible place yet.

They would need to start early—
start soon—

to have enough time
and they also needed
the entire town
to be distracted
to pull it off.

The festival was perfect.

Bell Lake has a spillway
like a waterfall.
The water is fast, furious,
but on the side is a blank
concrete wall.
A wall that can be seen
from the headquarters of
Bell Firearms.

It is there that Beck wants
to paint Helen—
Helen, who started a war.

When Beck suggested her
for the last mural,
Vivian said
She's perfect for Cassie.
The face that launched
ten thousand tweets.

What does it mean
for your body to be
the collateral
in a war you
never asked for?
I imagine it's how Helen felt
at the center of everything.

Beck comes early tonight.

The moment the sun
touches the horizon
she is out of the house
and running toward me.
Toward Betty.

She wrenches open the door,

and her eyes are wild
as they search the van.

I know she sees me
but her gaze moves on
still searching
and it takes me a moment
to realize:

She's looking for him.
He's not here.
I tell her what she
can see for herself.
I say the words out loud
because sometimes
you need to hear it.

Beck sinks to the ground
and she cries like I've
never seen.

Though maybe she cried
like this for me
and maybe her grandpa
held her tight.

But I can't hold her.
I can hover here
beside her.
I can reach out my arms
and hope that maybe
she feels the glance
of my touch on her shoulder,
but it is not the same
as wrapping your whole
self around someone

to keep them here,
to keep them from
breaking.

The screech of tires
draws my attention.
Vivian.

She barely stops the car,
is out and running
and falls down
beside her
and holds Beck
like Beck needs
to be held.

It is too much.
This loss.
It doesn't matter
that she knew it was coming,
grief leaves no room
for reason.

And for Beck, something else,
something ancient,
buried deep inside of her
alongside her bones.

Loneliness.

Beck has told us
in a million ways
the thing she feared most,
without ever having to
say it out loud.
She didn't want
to be alone.

Beck, always sharp
on her edges,
was hard to approach
but impossible
to walk away from.

I knew it
from the first moment,
and deep down,
Vivian knew it, too.
Knew they needed
each other.

We don't have to go,
says Vivian.
But Beck uses her sleeves
to wipe her tear-stained face.

Of course we do, *she says.*
We have to do this one.
I want Bell to see it.

When the sun sinks
into the earth behind them
I see only their dark
silhouettes against
an inferno sky.

We shouldn't have to do it—
set ourselves on fire
to change the way things are.

But I think maybe
to be a girl in this world
sometimes you have to burn.

Sometimes it's how
we light the way.

BECK

BECK WAS NO STRANGER TO GRIEF.

She knew it like she knew the night sky over the farmhouse in the summer. Like she knew the flecks of green in Cassie's blue eyes. Like she knew the twist of Vivian's braids, or the hot spark in her eyes when she was angry.

Like she knew the rise and fall of her grandpa's breath when she listened for it in his doorway at night.

Beck knew that grief could ruin her.

So she pushed it down, down deep. She let it settle in her bones, and she told it to stay there until she had the capacity to face it.

Tonight she had a job to do.

Vivian had begged Beck to call this one off. She knew Beck was hurting. And Beck knew Vivian was trying to help. But the only way through it, for Beck at least, was to keep moving.

He wasn't waiting in the van.

He didn't have unfinished business.

He was just there one moment, and gone the next.

If she let it, that would crush her.

Beck checked her backpack. This was a portrait, like the first one. Helen of Troy. Beck planned to do Cassie's profile this time, looking out to the sea, to the ships on the water. Coming to save her, by laying wreckage to a city.

They were on the far side of the lake, where the water went deepest, and where it spilled over the side of the levee, forming a thin veil of a waterfall. On the side of the levee, though, was a thirty-foot concrete wall, shoring it all up.

It was the perfect place. They'd been saving it for last because it was so visible. They needed the festival for coverage, distraction. And tonight they had it.

They drove in the dark, Beck going over a mental checklist of the tools she'd packed for tonight. They couldn't climb up the wall, so Beck would use rock-climbing ropes to rappell down it instead. It was more dangerous than anything else they'd done, but Beck didn't care. She had to see this through.

She hadn't even told him.

That was what hurt the most. She'd gotten the call days ago—she'd gotten the apprenticeship at the tattoo shop. She was going to move to the city and get an apartment. And try to be brave the way Cassie was brave. It was brave to *want* things for yourself. It was brave to go after them.

Beck knew her grandpa would have been proud of that decision.

And she never got to tell him.

"We should wait," Vivian said again. She wasn't letting up tonight, even with them standing on the top of the concrete wall, looping rope around the railings. Her hands worked to string the rope-pulley system they would use to lower Beck. They'd driven an hour away to a rock-climbing store for the materials, and watched tutorials online to learn how to use them properly. "This is dangerous."

The levee was old. Beck never noticed how decrepit it looked before now.

But the railings would hold her. They'd tested them.

"So was the water tower," Beck countered. She left the paint cans in her backpack, but put it on her front so she could reach them while she was in the air.

"That was nothing like this. And I thought you hated heights. Why don't we wait until—"

"We can't wait, V!" Beck shouted. She didn't want to argue with her. She wasn't changing her mind. They had to do this one. Mr. Bell was going to get away with it—with all of it—if they didn't keep up the pressure on all fronts. The podcast. The lawsuit.

And the murals.

"Why not?" Vivian asked.

"Because she's leaving us," Beck said. "That's why she's stronger, Vivian. Strong enough to leave the van. She's going to walk into those sunflowers, and she'll be gone for real this time."

"You don't know that," Vivian said. Beck looked up at her from her work.

"I do. And you know it, too. This might even be the last one. And this is the only time we can do it. With everyone and their brother and the *sheriff* at the Sunflower Festival."

She saw Vivian struggle with the truth of what she was saying.

Saw the moment she accepted it.

"Fine. Quickly. And please don't break your goddamn neck."

They secured the lines to the railing, and Vivian helped Beck climb over it to the other side. There was nothing behind Beck but a sheer drop into water, and she felt the start of panic in her chest.

She pushed that down, too.

Later.

Grieve later.

Panic later.

And there was something else driving Beck. Beyond grief, straight into this recklessness. The bruises on Cassie's neck were visible again. The more visible Cassie became to them, the more obvious her pain. Cassie was cold. She'd told them that, out by the sunflower field. Beck fixated on that.

Cassie was cold, and it was their job to help her.

But it was more than that. It was the thing that Beck had held inside all this time. Scared that saying it out loud would somehow hurt even worse than keeping the secret.

The last time Beck had taken things into her own hands, she'd gotten Cassie killed.

Beck remembered dropping Cassie at the hospital the day Nico went after her. Telling Vivian to stay in the waiting room, to wait for Cass. To call Beck if they needed a ride. And then she drove to Nico Bell's home. She parked Betty outside their gate, and climbed the wall, throwing her baseball bat over first.

She found Nico's car. It was new and sleek and stupid expensive.

Beck didn't care what kind of car it was. She cared that it was Nico's.

Beck smashed the windshield first, then the windows. She dented the sides and pulled out her keys to stab each of the car's tires. He came outside on the last tire, screaming. His whole face was red. Beck ran, slamming into the gate, and it opened enough for her to slip out just as Nico caught up to her. She wondered, as she ran, if this was the anger that Cassie had faced from him. If so, then the car hadn't been enough. She should have taken the bat to Nico himself.

But it was his words, as she ran back to Betty—his words screamed at Beck that haunted her now.

Even more than Cassie's ghost.

I warned you to stay out of this. I'll kill you.

And that's what Beck had lived with for five months.

Maybe he would have done it anyway. But Beck would always wonder if she'd been that breaking point. She'd wonder if he was looking for her that day at school.

And it was why Beck wouldn't—couldn't—stop until she finished this.

Beck stepped over the wall. She walked down it, one foot planted and then the next, moving backward. About ten feet down, she stopped. She saw the drawing in her mind, down to every last mark, and then she let her instinct guide her hands and form the first bold arcs on the wall. She painted Cassie's hair in curls tied on top of her head. Painted her eyes with the boldest blue paint Beck could find. Painted them fixated on the horizon, waiting for ships.

This was what Beck knew. The memory of Cassie's face. Her smile. She painted a flower in Cassie's hair. Finally, all that was left were the words. The same ones she'd painted onto every mural. *Collige Virgo Rosas.*

Beck reached for the last can of black paint. She had to move one of the ropes, and when she did she felt a tug, and dropped a few inches down the wall.

She looked up in the dark, her eyes adjusting to make out the railing above.

It was bending.

Vivian saw it at the same moment, reached for the rope that tethered Beck to the wall.

But the railing gave out before she got there.

Beck plummeted to the water below.

The water wasn't deep.

Beck knew that because she cracked her head against the bottom of the levee when she hit it.

And then it felt like time stopped, and she was moving in slow motion. She knew it was bad. Knew she'd drown. But it already felt so far away, like it was happening to someone else.

Like she was watching a movie, black and white and crackling.

And then everything was illuminated.

Bright lights pierced the water, and she could see the long strands of her red hair fanning out all around her. Her hand was reaching for the surface, but it might as well have been a hundred feet instead of three.

Her vision was going dark—cloudy with the pain. Cloudy with the muddy redness filling the water around her.

Not her hair, after all.

Blood.

But those lights were still on her—from somewhere up above.

They were coming for her.

Not Vivian or Cass, but someone she'd waited for her whole life.

Those bright lights could only be otherworldly. Something she had looked for in the night sky, again and again, wishing to be stolen away and taken to some other galaxy, some other life.

And here they were.

Coming for her.

Finally.

VIVIAN

VIVIAN RAN DOWN THE SIDE OF the levee, screaming for Beck as she went.

"Cass, lights! I need light."

The headlights of the van flickered on, illuminating the surface of the water.

She could see the shape of Beck in the water.

Vivian jumped in. She swam for the spot she'd seen Beck a moment ago, diving in, arms outstretched.

There. Vivian's fingers tangled in Beck's hair, and she dove farther, wrapping her arms around Beck and dragging her back to the surface. Vivian pulled her to the side of the levee, out of the water. Beck wasn't breathing. Vivian started CPR. She'd done this before, a hundred times, in training, and in emergencies. She'd brought people back before, and goddammit, she would do it again.

She counted. Breathed for Beck. Did a chest compression. Began again.

It couldn't have been more than a minute, though it felt like an eternity to Vivian.

Beck sputtered, choked. Began to cough up the water.

When Vivian sat back to give her space, she tugged her own hair out of the way, and realized then that her hands were covered in blood.

Beck's head was bleeding. A lot.

Vivian needed help.

She managed to get Beck up to her feet. She couldn't hold her weight entirely, but with Beck leaning against her and her arm wrapped around Vivian, they stumbled up to the van.

Vivian moved Beck into the middle seat, lying down, and immediately grabbed a sweatshirt from the seat to apply pressure to the wound on Beck's head.

She looked at Beck's blood all over her hands, and suddenly Vivian was back in that classroom. Three gunshots and it was over. Cassie was gone before Vivian even registered what was happening. Vivian's hands were covered in blood.

Vivian hadn't known she'd been shot, too, until someone tried to figure out how to tie a tourniquet on her leg. They were doing it wrong. They weren't tying it tight enough.

Vivian talked them through it, staring down at her hands the whole time. It wasn't her blood. It was Cassie's. Vivian remembered waking in the hospital after Cassie died. It felt like the world had ended. As far as Vivian was concerned, the world did end that day. And then everyone acted like it was a normal thing, to lose someone you love to a bullet at school. And Vivian had been full of anger from that moment on. Anger that this was a version of the world she was expected to accept and live with. To not be consumed by her loss. To not think that their lives were worth the battle—against Bell, against the company, against anyone who didn't know who Cassie was. So she'd fought.

But tonight took her back to that day, only this time it wasn't Cassie's blood on her hands, it was Beck's.

And Vivian couldn't breathe.

Not her, too, was all she could think. *Not Beck, too.*

Vivian was frozen in place, but she felt the hum of the engine starting. She looked up and found Cassie in the driver's seat.

That snapped her out of it a bit.

"Cassie," Vivian started. "Can you—"

"I think so," Cass said. "I can feel the pedals. I can feel the wheel. Where do we go?"

"We need Matteo. He's not working tonight. Go to his house. I'll call him on the way."

Cassie pulled the gear shift, and the van started to move. Vivian stayed where she was, her chest tight with fear and shock, her hands slick with the wetness of blood as she tried to stop the bleeding from the gash on Beck's head. Beck was quiet, but conscious. She kept squeezing Vivian's hand in reassurance.

"Hurry," Vivian said, a whispered plea.

The van surged forward, and Cassie's hands slipped right through the steering wheel. It began to veer off course, heading for the ditch on the side of the road, but Cassie swore under her breath, and put her hands back in place.

She grabbed the steering wheel, corrected course.

And then they were driving.

Cassie drove them back through Bell.

It was late, and there was no one else out on the streets.

Cassie picked up speed on the next turn. They weren't far from Vivian's home. They turned onto the street.

And then Cassie's hands slipped through the wheel again, and Betty turned hard and fast, veering sharply right. The tree line was too close.

And once again it felt like the world was ending.

Vivian sat in Matteo's kitchen with Beck's head on her lap.

He'd heard the tires screech when Cassie slammed on the brakes, trying to stop in time. But she couldn't, and Betty had bounced off a tree before rolling to a stop on the side of the road.

Matteo had come outside at the noise and sprang into action. He had ushered Vivian into his house, carrying Beck.

They'd worked at his family's kitchen table, using his first aid kit to stitch up Beck's head. Vivian held her even after Matteo was done and started to clean up.

Beck began to stir, her eyelashes fluttering. "I'm here," Vivian whispered. "You'll be okay. You scared the hell out of me, Tribeca Jones."

Beck's eyes opened, narrowed on her.

"Don't call me that," she said. She looked around the kitchen. "So no aliens?"

"What?" Vivian asked.

"She might need that hospital visit, Vivian," Matteo said from the doorway. Vivian glanced up at him. He leaned on the doorframe, not forcing the issue, just suggesting the idea.

"S'a joke," Beck murmured. "Aliens. Joke."

Beck started to sit up, and Vivian helped her.

"What happened?" she asked.

"Cassie crashed your van," Vivian said. "It's outside, a little beat-up."

"And Cass?"

"Still there," Vivian said. "But I don't think for long."

"I know," Beck said. "We need to get back to her."

"Your head okay?" Matteo stepped forward, checking Beck's stitches.

"Barely even hurts," Beck said.

"Liar." Matteo laughed. "Let's go see what damage that hideous van of yours suffered. See if we can get you out of here before someone calls the cops and this whole thing blows up in our faces."

Vivian helped Beck stand, and then she and Matteo both

looped arms around her, but Beck shook her head, pushed them off.

Insisted she could walk on her own.

"I told you we should have just burned something down."

Vivian laughed softly. Beck *had* said that, right at the start.

"Well, when you're right, you're right," Vivian said. "That would have been easier."

It was enough. Tonight was enough to make Vivian understand that they'd hit the limit of what they could do on their own to fight Bell. And Cassie knew it, too. She'd been trying to tell them, and it was Vivian who had refused to listen. She'd been selfish, now holding on to Cassie just because she couldn't say goodbye.

But it was time.

Time to say goodbye to Cass before someone else got hurt.

CASSIE

Beck's hands are
covered in paint,
Vivian's are
covered in blood.

Vivian limps,
and Beck leans
against Matteo.

I feel a deep,
guttural
thud
in my chest
right where my
heart used to be
at the sight of Beck,
conscious,
alive.

There was a moment,
after she fell
and was lying
at the bottom of the levee,
underwater.
The moment Vivian
dragged her out
and looked up
at Betty and me
and when our
eyes met
I knew beyond a doubt
we thought the same thing:
Not Beck, too.

We won't finish
the Helen mural
but I think that's okay.

I think we can say
we did our best.

I know I can say
my friends fought for me.
Matteo leans in,
whispers something

to them just outside
and Vivian looks up
startled,
but she nods.

Matteo approaches
the van alone
and climbs into
the passenger seat.

He doesn't turn around
when he talks.

Hey, Cass, *he says.*
My name catches
and he clears his
throat, roughly.

V and Beck, well,
they say you are here,
sort of trapped?

I don't know.
I don't know
what I believe
anymore, *he says.*

I move into the middle seat
so I'm hovering just behind him.
Beck's phone is on the floor
and I reach down
to push a button
and it lights up

It's Beck's first mural
filling the screen.
Cassandra, who saw the future.
That mural always
makes me think the same thing.
If only seeing it coming had
been enough to stop it.

Oh, hey there, *Matteo says,*
looking down at the phone.
Was that you?
He smiles when
I press the button
once more.

Cass, here's the thing,
he says. I miss you—
I know it was new,
not gonna pretend
I had any claim on you.

I smile at the words
said so easily.
If only all boys
could be more like Matteo
and less like Nico.

But I know what claim
you had on me.
And I'll spend forever
thinking, If only.
If only I'd gotten
to her first.

I think you being here,
if you're really here,
Matteo says, shifting
in his seat,
peering back,
right through me,
is the closest thing
to a miracle
I'll ever see.

The three of you—
well, you're fucking crazy,
you know that, right?
But you're also my heroes.

It's making a difference,
the murals, this town,
everyone is talking
about you, about guns,
about how it got that far.

But Beck could have died tonight
and the police—
they're gonna find them,
eventually.
If they don't get hurt,
they'll be arrested.

Matteo opens the door,
and it protests loudly,
having just been crashed
against a tree.
Then he pops his head
back in through the window,
goofy smile on his face.

Love you, Cass.
I should have said that
when you were here,
but I'm glad
I can tell you now.

Goodbye, Matteo, *I say.*
But of course,
he doesn't hear me.

Matteo didn't have
to tell me
what I had already
figured out for myself,
standing at the edge of the
sunflower fields
feeling the tug and pull.
It calls me.

And then tonight,
watching, helpless to stop it,
when Beck slipped and fell.

Matteo only said out loud
what I had known
for some time.
But sometimes
you need to hear it.

As long as I am here,
they'll never stop.

WE CAN BE HEROES
SEASON 2: EPISODE 20
"THE CEO"

MERIT: I'm glad you could make it to *We Can Be Heroes*, Mr. Bell. I've been looking forward to having you on here for a long time.

BELL: And I hope this marks the conclusion of your series on Bell, Ms. Logan. I'm sure you're ready to move on to bigger things than our little town.

MERIT: With the coverage it's getting, there is nothing bigger than this town right now. But why don't we back up a little first. Tell me about Cassie.

BELL: She was a troubled girl. An actress. Dramatic. She was always starting fights with Nico. We—my wife and I—tried to get Nico to break it off, but those kids were in too deep. It was a volatile relationship.

MERIT: Volatile. As in violent?

BELL: As in unstable.

MERIT: Then why push back on the protection order? It would have distanced them, at least.

BELL: With my son at fault. That was unacceptable.

MERIT: Is that why you went to the hospital to keep Cassie from filing? To protect Nico?

BELL: What?

MERIT: You went with Sheriff Thomas to the hospital on March thirteenth.

[Extended silence]

MERIT: Mr. Bell?

BELL: . . . You don't have proof of that.

MERIT: You don't know that.

BELL: It doesn't matter. She filed her paperwork. She got the order. In the end, none of that mattered.

MERIT: So you don't think Bell Firearms, the way it advertised, the culture Nico grew up in, your disdain for Cassie Queen—none of that influenced Nico?

BELL: I don't think anything we did could have changed the outcome. It is what it is.

MERIT: Mr. Bell, did you have faith that your company could handle any backlash after the shooting?

BELL: The company has faced many hardships in its two hundred years, of course.

MERIT: But this wasn't *really* a hardship, was it? Not politically. Are you aware that gun sales spike in the aftermath of school shootings?

BELL: I am aware.

MERIT: So, in a way, aren't you profiting directly off these shootings?

BELL: Now, listen, people get scared. They reach for—

MERIT: Safety. You promise them *safety*, Mr. Bell.

BELL: That's right.

MERIT: Did you promise Cassie that safety, too?

BELL: Cassie Queen wasn't my responsibility.

MERIT: That's cold, Mr. Bell.

BELL: Hang on a damn second. I lost my son, too.

MERIT: And I'm sorry for your loss, but your son was a killer. And Cassie was scared of him. You knew that, didn't you? When you went to the hospital that day. You saw how he hurt her.

BELL: No one could have guessed what would happen next.

MERIT: But that's not the truth, Mr. Bell. All the warning signs were there. Plus access to weapons. But you and the sheriff still believe that ignoring Cassie was justified even though, as it turned out, she was completely right to be scared . . . because in your experience, what? Cassie was lying? Overreacting?

BELL: Not lies. Exaggerations. Dramatization of the truth. I've seen it my whole life.

MERIT: You don't just mean Cassie, do you?

BELL: Of course I do. Ms. Logan, why do *you* care so much?

MERIT: I'm surprised, Steven. I thought if you got on a call with me you'd at least recognize my voice.

[Long pause]

BELL: Who the hell—Logan. *Hannah* Logan.

MERIT: Merit is my middle name. I started using it after your PR team followed me to college and I had to transfer. Twice.

BELL: . . . Christ. This whole thing was a setup.

MERIT: That sounds a little . . . how did you describe Cassie again? *Dramatic.* Steven, I know you have five decades

328

of experiences telling you that everything is about you, but that's not actually true. I'm here for Cassie. But I couldn't miss the opportunity to tell you directly that you are scum.

BELL: You thought you were in love with me.

MERIT: And you took advantage of the situation. I was seventeen.

BELL: It doesn't matter. You can't touch me.

MERIT: All I have to do is tell my story. And you started it by joining me today for this interview. The only name I've never named on here is yours. But that will change, next week, unless—

BELL: Unless what?

MERIT: Stop intimidating the Queens and Vivian Hughes. Drop the reward for the muralists. If you keep going after them, I'll tell my story publicly. I'll release the second half of this interview. When I was a teen, I was scared into silence. And I know you tried to do the same to Cassie. I'll be damned if there's no accountability for you *again*.

BELL: No one will believe you.

MERIT: Eight years ago that was true. No one believed me. But with everything we know about Cassie—the way you ignored Nico's violence, tried to shut Cassie up . . . I think now they would believe me. Do you really want to take the chance?

BELL: . . . I'll drop the reward. You'll keep your silence.

MERIT: For now. It won't matter soon, anyway.

BELL: Why's that?

MERIT: Because that lawsuit is going to destroy you, even without my help.

[Phone call disconnects]

MURAL 7

TITLE: **THE FATES**

LOCATION: **THE BARN**

CASSIE

Vivian and Beck
come back to me
a little bruised
and a little broken
and I can't help but think,
Now that makes
three of us.

Suddenly
the only thing I want
in this
whole,
wide,
terrifying
world
is to keep my friends safe.

Beck gets Betty started.
She's hurt,
but she's moving.
Not unlike Beck herself,
who climbs into
the passenger seat
for once, letting V drive.

Vivian, *I say,*
trying to get her attention
while she drives.
Vivian, it's time.
I have to go.

No, *says Vivian.*

She answers too fast.
like she knew
what I was going to say,
and she keeps her eyes
on the road.

Beck turns to me.
Now? *she asks.*
But I just lost him.

You found someone, too,
I tell her, my eyes
going back to Vivian.

They're both quiet
for so long
I think they'll just ignore me.

Where? *Vivian asks.*

The sunflowers, *Beck says,*
answering for me.
Answering like she's known
for some time, too.
Like she's been watching me
watch those flowers,
like she knew
I was listening
to something inside.

We drive through town
and the remains
of the festival
are still there.
Sunflowers
on sunflowers

on sunflowers.
On signs
and lampposts,
painted onto
storefronts
except the one
that's boarded up still,
because someone
threw a brick
through the window.

August is the only time
that Bell talks about flowers
instead of guns,
and I think it's the perfect time
to say goodbye.

We park on the edge
of Beck's grandpa's
property.
Now Beck's property,
I guess.
Right up against the field.

It's too late and too early,
that witching hour of

dark, while you wait
for the sun.

So we wait together.
Vivian and Beck
climb into the back seat,
one on either side of me.

Why do you think this happened?
Vivian asks, like it only just now
dawned on her to ask me.

I think we were wrong,
I tell them,
The unfinished business?
It wasn't vengeance.

Then what the hell was it?
asks Vivian.

It was you.
You needed to find
your way back to this.
I gesture to the three of us.
Maybe you two just
really needed me

for a little longer,
I say.

And now we don't?
Beck asks.

No, *I tell her.*
You'll have each other.

The sky slips through
its colors, first pitch-black
and heavy with stars,
then a grayish blue, then
finally, the first pink streaks of light.

This could be any morning,
the three of us
piling into Betty together.
The same as always.

And when their arms
wrap around me,
I feel them.

The weight of their bodies
press up against mine

like I'm solidly here
for just a moment more.

Hey, Beck, *I say.*

What? *she whispers,*
leaning her head
on my shoulder.
The same as always.

I changed my mind,
I whisper back.
I think the real reason
I came back
was just to crash
your crappy van.

Beck laughs, and her laugh
starts mine,
and mine gets to Vivian,
the same as always.

And even now, after
all the hurt,
or maybe in spite of it,
the three of us are

just as we began:
made of laughter
and light,
our summers
endless before us.

And we've gathered
all the roses
our arms can bear.

BECK

THE VERY LAST MURAL WASN'T FOR anyone but them.

It was the three Fates. Beck painted it on the side of the barn in the last week of August. Those last days spent painting were long and lonely. But she wouldn't be lonely for long.

Beck had designed this last one for Vivian. It was the three of them together. And crossing in between them, tying them together, were the strands of fate, being woven into a tapestry all their own. Beck liked the idea of it—of invisible strings tying her to the people she loved most. Keeping them close, even when they were so far away. Even when they were out of sight.

She painted Vivian's braids, and that constantly furrowed brow. She painted her leaning over the tapestry, examining their work. Ever critical. Ever put-together. Beck painted herself with her red curls all over, and with the strands twirled around her fingers, tangled a bit. Doing her best to keep up. *Trying.*

341

And then Cassie, with the string in her hands and flowers where her hair ought to be. Every kind of flower Beck could think of, gathered like a massive crown around her head and shoulders. And one last string, weaving between the three of them. Tying them to each other.

Beck heard tires on the driveway and stepped down from her ladder as the car came into view. Merit Logan climbed out of her car. She walked up beside Beck, hand over her eyes to block out the brightness of the sun so she could see the mural clearly.

"That's the best one yet," she told Beck.

They walked into the garage together, and Merit pulled out her phone. She'd promised Beck that she could listen to the interview with Steven Bell before it aired.

"Are you going to post the whole thing?" Beck asked when she finished listening.

"Unsure," Merit said. "I might let him sit with the threat of it. See what he does next. I just want to give the Queens and Vivian some protection while this lawsuit gets off the ground."

"He dropped the reward," Beck said.

"I heard." Merit smiled. "It's something. But I'm leaving Bell to finish my last few episodes of the season. A few more interviews, but I don't need to be here anymore. And I guess you don't either? Vivian told me you're leaving." Merit tucked her phone away. She gestured to the shop. "What about this?"

Beck shrugged. "It will be here. It's mine. If I need it. But right now, I need something else."

"You need to move on," Merit said.

"I'm going to the city. I got a job. I'll apprentice at a tattoo shop there for a while. See where that leads."

"And Vivian?"

"We're getting a place together," Beck said. "She couldn't . . . she didn't want to be in a dorm."

"You both are going to do amazing things," Merit said.

"Thanks," Beck said. "And thank you for . . ." Beck trailed off. She'd never been good with this kind of thing.

"I should thank you," Merit said. "It's the closure I needed. You want to hear something ridiculous? I originally came back here because of Cassie, because I thought—don't laugh—I thought she was haunting me."

Merit held up her hand when Beck did laugh softly. *If only you knew*, Beck thought.

"I know. Ridiculous. Anyway, I *swear* I could see her in my dreams. A young woman, with long dark hair. Asking me for help. But this past week? I could finally see that face in my dreams. And it was me. She was the younger version of me. That one I'd hidden away from the world. Whose trauma I thought I could bury and forget. But that's not how trauma works, is it?"

"No," Beck said. "I don't think it is."

"I thought I was here to help Cassie. To tell her story. But really it was to tell mine, too. I needed to talk about Bell."

They walked into the sunlight together, facing the sunflower field. Cassie's field, as Beck thought of it now.

"And now?" Beck asked Merit.

"I'll post this interview tonight. I don't even need the second half of it yet—he went to the hospital. Tried to scare Cassie. Had the sheriff answering to him. That's enough. For now."

"Good. Take the bastards down."

"Take care of yourself, Beck. And take care of Vivian."

"I will," Beck said, and she knew she could do that. That's who she was. She took care of people. Even if it couldn't be forever.

After Merit drove away, Beck retraced her steps, back into the garage, and set Betty's keys on the workbench. They'd discussed taking the van to the city, but it felt so empty now, without Cassie's voice echoing through it.

Beck heard a car pull up outside, and the chirp of a horn.

She hung the Closed sign on the door on her way out. Beck threw her bags into Vivian's back seat and climbed into the passenger seat. She didn't look back at the farm or the barn or even Betty as they drove away.

It was like the stars on overcast nights. It was like Cassie stepping into those sunflower fields one last time.

Everything she loved was still there, even if she couldn't see it.

VIVIAN

"NOW WHERE ARE WE GOING?" BECK asked when Vivian turned in the opposite direction of the highway.

"One last stop," Vivian said, smiling at Beck's impatience to leave Bell—something she never thought she'd see. But it had been Beck's idea for them to leave together.

The lawsuits could take years, Beck had argued. And Vivian didn't want to be around every time there was a development that left the town on edge, did she?

So Vivian said yes, and called her college, accepted their offer to take a class at a time while she went to therapy to help her deal with everything. One little step at a time. And Matteo would be in the same city as them. They'd have a familiar face, a friend in the crowd. It was a chance to start again. And they all really needed that.

Vivian's hand brushed the bandage on her thigh as she drove. She'd insisted on being Beck's first tattoo in her apprenticeship. They'd chosen a familiar design—Beck was still learning, and the tattoo had to work around the scar tissue on her leg. It was the same thing Beck had painted on Cassie's leg last summer—a sunflower in full bloom, and underneath it, Cassie's favorite words. *Collige Virgo Rosas.*

"You wanted this to say 'YOLO,' right?" Beck had teased her over the buzz of the tattoo needle when she did it.

Vivian turned down the side road that led to the lake.

Before they were allowed to swim without supervision, they'd meet at the massive willow tree that grew on the hill overlooking the water. Vivian's mom and Cassie's parents would drop them off in the morning, and not come back for them until nightfall. They were free to roam all day. Their summers had always been like that—entirely their own.

The willow was a monster these days, overgrown and unkempt, curling in upon itself. Its long solitude evident in the tangled-ness of its branches.

But this tree wasn't always so lonely.

They used to spend hours in its shade, summer warm on their skin and lips tart from the green apples they'd stolen from the Warrens' orchards nearby. If they sat long enough, and still enough, they could track the way the sunflowers craned their necks, following the sun as it set.

Back then, the willow's branches would move in the wind like seaweed in waves. Tug and release. Back and forth, the ends tickling their bare legs. But today those branches were snarled in a way that made it hard for Vivian, pulling Beck

346

along with her, to climb over and between them to get to the tree.

She put her hand out and ran her fingers along the surface of the tree, searching for the heart of the thing. It took a while; it was nearly invisible after so many years, covered by time and the tree's other scars.

"Remember, we would sit *just there*, facing west to look out over the fields and the lake."

"I remember," Beck said.

They'd stay until the bluest of days collapsed into pink.

And then they'd wait while the whole universe appeared above them in the dark, in fistfuls of stars at a time, until they were overwhelmed by the number of them. They thought it was all for them.

Beck reached into her overalls and pulled out a pocket-knife. "Here, you do the honors."

When Vivian's fingers found the carved heart, she brushed over the letters of their names inside of it. She could hear Cassie's voice with each beat of her own heart, her pulse so strong in her fingertips that it was like the weathered shape on the tree was the thing throbbing. She took the blade from Beck, thanking her softly. She sank the knife into the willow's bark and pulled down. Cutting was easier that direction, and she wasn't trying to take her fingers off.

They must have been ten or eleven years old when they first carved the heart and their names into the tree, and

Vivian didn't remember it being this difficult to cut. Then again, it would have been Beck who did the carving. Vivian wouldn't have dared.

The tree was younger then. Maybe it used to be softer, its bark more supple.

They were softer then, too.

She finished retracing the heart and their initials, and Vivian tried to recall the exact day they'd put it there, but they all ran together in her memory now. It would have been a bright, sun-soaked day. Any one of a thousand they'd shared together.

"All right, we should go," Vivian said, returning the knife to Beck. "We need to pick up our keys to the apartment before the office closes."

But Beck was facing the lake. She turned and smiled at Vivian. "One last jump?"

Vivian knew that soon the leaves would change color on the trees. The apples in the orchard would be plucked, the rotten ones left on the ground for the deer. The sunflowers would be harvested or left to wither. Autumn would come, and summer, it turned out, didn't last forever. But every memory that Vivian had of Cassie and Beck was flooded by sunshine.

When the three of them were together, their summer was infinite.

WE CAN BE HEROES
SEASON 3: EPISODE 25
"THE SURVIVOR"

[Audio clip]

VIVIAN HUGHES: What Congresswoman Roberts is proposing would mean real change in the way we respond to relationship violence. We are relieved that, at least in some way, what happened to Cassie is being acknowledged. This legislation, if passed—and please, call your representatives and let them know you support it—would keep someone else safe. Cassie deserved so much more. But we are holding her memory close while we fight for these changes. Fight to protect the next girl.

MERIT LOGAN: Welcome back, listeners, to We Can Be Heroes. *It's hard to believe that we are starting our third season of the podcast. Thank you for listening. For believing survivors' stories. You just heard from Vivian Hughes, Cassandra Queen's friend and a survivor of the shooting that took Cassie's life. Vivian is also part of the lawsuit aimed at Bell Firearms.*

Last summer, we told the story of Bell through a series of interviews. At that time, the entire town was caught up in the gun control debate, its own tragic history with a school shooting, and a series of vigilante art pieces targeting Bell Firearms in Cassie's name.

At the conclusion of those events, we saw the sheriff of Bell step down in disgrace following a public outcry over his gross mishandling of Cassie Queen's case and his direct collaboration with her abuser's father, Steven Bell. Shortly after that, Mr. Bell resigned from his position as CEO of Bell Firearms.

We are still tracking two lawsuits related to these events, a civil suit in which Steven Bell is expected to settle, and another against the company itself. Last Tuesday, the Supreme Court of the United States agreed to hear the case against Bell Firearms. The outcome of this case could change the landscape of gun violence culpability going forward.

And lastly, as Vivian Hughes just referenced, Congresswoman Maria Roberts recently announced new legislation that calls for sweeping gun reform and protections for survivors of domestic violence. This legislation restricts firearm access, strengthens protection orders, funds new research on gun violence, and establishes a national PSA campaign on teen dating violence to increase awareness.

The title of this legislation is the Cassandra Amendment.

CASSIE

I am running
through a field
of sunflowers
(and I think,
perhaps,
it goes on forever).

The sun is warm
on my shoulders,
and I'll gladly stay
in this summer
forever.

Or at least
until my friends
can meet me.

Vivian is the no
to Beck's yes
and from the time
I am eight
they keep me in check.

In my childhood, they are
the vibration of tires
on a long stretch of highway.
The soundtrack,
the white noise,
the familiar hum.

They are mechanical
and reassuring,
even after hundreds
of miles together,
because if the tires are moving,
then you haven't crashed,
or gotten lost,
or stranded yourself somewhere.

It means you are going
the right way.
And I always was,
with them.

And I know,
maybe better than most,
that life isn't all laughter
and it isn't all sunshine,
but thanks to Vivian and Beck
I also know that
a lot of the time it is.

My memories of them
are push and pull.
And always,
one is the honey
to the other's sting.

They are the inverse
of each other,
as necessary as inhale, exhale.
They only needed
the reminder.

I wonder if maybe
all along,
they were balancing
the whole world
the way they balanced
each other, and me.

Maybe they kept
everything
in check, riding
on overburdened shoulders,
and the simple belief
that evil men
should face
consequences.

And if you'd laugh
at the thought of three girls
being at the center
of absolutely everything,
I would say
that you obviously
haven't met any girls.

If you don't know
Beck's humor, or Vivian's grace.
Their riotous, righteous anger.
That's what girls
are made of.

I would know, because I've seen it
and because, for a brief time,
I was made of
all those things, too.

And I have also seen
the way they bent time
and space, like their grief
held a gravity
that could not be denied.
And when it gave in,
the strangest thing happened.
It let me come back to them,
for a time, perhaps just
long enough
to remind the world
what we girls are capable of.
Like when Cassandra
saw the future,
when Ariadne
escaped the maze,
when Circe cursed the men,
and Helen started a war,
when Medusa was hunted,
and Andromeda was sacrificed
for her city.

If you already know
the truth about girls
(if you've been lucky enough
to see it)
then you already know

it is possible for three girls
to be at the center
of their own stories—
to be at the center
of everything.

You already know that
we can be heroes.

ACKNOWLEDGMENTS

THE PODCAST IN THIS BOOK WAS inspired by the Take Back the Night rallies that I first attended (in awe and gratitude) and later organized on my college campus. A lot of my feelings from that experience are woven into this story—empathy for fellow survivors, frustration with the systems that failed us again and again . . . and anger. Anger that we needed rallies at all to be heard. Anger that we needed to gather in numbers to feel safe.

I've listened to hundreds of stories from survivors of violence, as an advocate, a counselor, a friend. And the thing that always struck me was the echo in the room. There was the trauma itself, infuriating on its own, and then there was the follow up: not being believed. Living with a fear that is never quite taken seriously enough.

This book is for everyone who shares their stories anyway. It can be incredibly scary to do that. But it makes the world a little safer every single time. Every single story. *We Can Be Heroes* is just one story. And it's fictional. But the heart of it is the most true thing I've learned: we get to be the heroes of our own stories.

I know that sophomore novels are notoriously difficult, but writing this book in a global pandemic was a particular challenge. Now that I'm on the other side of it, I'm not surprised that I wrote a story about grief and anger and how it can shape us into new people.

But I'm also not surprised that I wrote a book about friendship, and how it endures. I'm so grateful for the incredible network of family and friends who found ways to encourage and support me this year—despite long distances, and without ever seeing each other in person. Thank you, Jenny Perinovic, for cheering me on in my writing journey for almost a decade now. Your friendship means the world to me. I've been so lucky to make new friends in the writing community this year who are deeply kind and thoughtful and generous. Thank you, Dante, Rocky, Liz, Alex, and Nora. What an unexpected gift out of an awful year.

Thank you to my wonderful agent, Suzie Townsend, for being the best advocate for my books (and for me). Thank you to everyone at New Leaf Literary—your passion for your authors is unmatched. I'm so grateful to Katherine Tegen for helping my stories find such an incredible home. A huge thank you in particular to: Jessica Berg, Gwen Morton, Joel Tippie, Amy Ryan, Kristen Eckhardt, Lisa Calcasola, and Aubrey Churchward for their work on *Heroes*; Samantha

Mash, for creating the stunning cover for this book; and Tanu Srivastava, for answering my many questions and being so gracious about them. And finally, thank you to my editor, Ben Rosenthal, for your incredible insight, and for helping me dig through the messy early drafts of this story and find the heart of it. It's really such an honor to work with you.

I'm so grateful to my mom, who continues to find a million new ways to tell me she believes in me. Who taught me to love books in the first place by always having one in her hands. Thank you for setting the example for me, on how to love books and how to be a mom. I'm very thankful for my dad, who always believed that art was worth pursuing just for the sake of it, and taught us to believe the same. Thank you for encouraging me to love music and lyrics, my first early attempts at writing.

And lastly, thank you Jackson, Kayleigh, Katharyn, and Andrew, for being my earliest readers and my best friends. I'm so incredibly lucky to have you. Rowan and Theo, thank you for leaving me sweet notes slid under doors, left in my notebooks, stuck to the walls of our home, and on the keyboard of my laptop, and for being the absolute greatest joys of my life.

RESOURCES

We Can Be Heroes is about the worst that can happen in an unhealthy relationship. It's about warning signs missed and a life stolen. But there are so many organizations doing incredible work to provide people with an entirely different outcome for their own stories. If you would like to learn more about intimate partner violence, organizations dedicated to reducing gun violence, and the laws impacting these issues, resources are listed below. Please remember that abusers can track activity, and only access these websites from a safe device and location.

The National Domestic Violence Hotline: Advocates are available 24/7/365 to answer calls and provide information and resources. The website has a live chat feature to message with an advocate, an escape button if you need to quickly exit, and Spanish translation. www.thehotline.org
1-800-799-7233
1-800-787-3224 (TTY)

Love Is Respect: Highly trained advocates offer information and support for young people experiencing dating violence. Also provides resources for concerned family members, friends, teachers, counselors, service providers, or members of law enforcement. Free and confidential phone and texting services, available 24/7. This website has an escape button, live chat feature, and Spanish translation. www.loveisrespect.org

1-800-331-9474
1-866-331-8453 (TTY)
Text: "loveis" to 22522

National Coalition Against Domestic Violence: Provides education, advocacy, policy, and resources related to domestic violence. Hosts "Action Alerts" to help users engage in policy action calls for legislation and VAWA renewal, including graphics and suggested language to use on social media to raise awareness and call political figures to action. www.ncadv.org

Everytown for Gun Safety: Researches causes of and solutions for gun violence. Provides advocacy and grassroots coalition building by state. Helps elect gun sense candidates. Demands accountability for gun violence. www.everytown.org

Sandy Hook Promise: Establishes education, research, advocacy, and organizing to end school shootings and protect children from acts of violence in their homes, communities, and schools. www.sandyhookpromise.org